CW00727166

Enid Blyton's Story Book TREASURY

THE ENID BLYTON TRUST
FOR CHILDREN

We hope you will enjoy this book. Please think for a moment about those children who are too ill to do the exciting things you and your friends do.

Help them by sending a donation, large or small, to THE ENID BLYTON TRUST FOR CHILDREN. The Trust will use all your gifts to help children who are sick or handicapped and need to be made happy and comfortable.

Please send your postal order or cheque to:
The Enid Blyton Trust for Children,
Bedford House,
3 Bedford Street,
London WC2E 9HD

Thank you very much for your help.

The Enid Blyton Newsletter

Would you like to receive The Enid Blyton Newsletter? It has lots of news about Enid Blyton books, videos, plays, etc. There are also puzzles and a page for your letters. It is published three times a year and is free for children who live in the United Kingdom and Ireland.

If you would like to receive it for a year, please write to: The Enid Blyton Newsletter, PO Box 357, London WC2E 9HQ sending your name and address. (UK and Ireland only.)

Enid Blyton's Story Book TREASURY

DEAN

First published 1988
This edition published 1993 by Dean,
an imprint of Reed Consumer Books Limited,
Michelin House, 81 Fulham Road, London SW3 6RB
and Auckland, Melbourne, Singapore and Toronto

Stories copyright © Darrell Waters Limited 1963, 1964, 1965, 1966
Illustrations copyright © Reed International Books Limited 1988

ISBN 0 603 55227 7

Enid Blyton is a registered trademark of Darrell Waters Limited

A CIP catalogue record for this title is available from the British Library

This book is sold subject to the condition that it shall not, by way of trade or otherwise, be lent, resold, hired out, or otherwise circulated without the publisher's prior consent in any form of binding or cover other than that in which it is published and without a similar condition including this condition being imposed on the subsequent purchaser

Produced by Mandarin Offset

Printed in China

The stories in this book previously appeared in *Enid Blyton's Chimney Corner, Book of Fairies, Brer Rabbit Again, Brer Rabbit's A Rascal, Happy Hours, Round the Clock Stories, Stories for Bedtime, Story Time Book, Sunshine Book, Tales of Toyland*

Contents

Mr. Grumpygroo's Hat

Mr. Grumpygroo was the crossest old man in the whole of Tweedle village. No one had ever seen him smile, or hear him laugh. He was so mean that he saved all his crumbs and made them into a pudding instead of giving them to the birds.

Of course, as you can guess, no one liked him. No one smiled at old Grumpygroo, or said good morning. They frowned at him, or scowled, for no village likes to have such a crosspatch living in it. Grumpygroo didn't seem to mind. He lived all alone in his tumble-down cottage, and made friends with no one.

But he was very lonely. He often wished the children would smile at him as they smiled at the Balloon-Woman and Mr. Sooty, the sweep. But they never did, and old Grumpygroo vowed and declared he wouldn't be the first to smile at anyone, not he!

Every day he went walking through the village with his old green scarf round his neck, and his old top-hat on his head; and he might have gone on scowling and frowning for ever, if something strange hadn't happened.

One morning he went into the hall to fetch his scarf and his hat. It was rather a dark day, and old Grumpygroo could hardly see. He felt about for his scarf, and tied it round his neck. Then he groped about for his hat.

There was a lamp, unlighted, standing in the hall on the chest where Grumpygroo usually stood his hat. On it was a lamp-shade made of yellow silk with a fringe of coloured beads. By mistake Mr. Grumpygroo took up the shade instead of his hat. It was so dark that he didn't see the mistake he had made, and he put the lamp-shade on his head! It felt rather like his top-hat, so he didn't notice any difference; and out he walked into the street wearing a bright yellow lamp-shade instead of his old hat.

He looked very funny indeed, for all the beads shook as he walked. Just as he went out of his gate, the clouds fled, the sun came out and all the birds began to sing. It was a perfectly lovely spring day.

Even old Mr. Grumpygroo felt a little bit glad, and he half wished he had a friend who would smile at him. But he knew nobody would, so he set his face into a scowl, and went down the street.

The first person he met was the jolly Balloon-Woman carrying her load of

balloons. As soon as she saw the yellow lamp-shade on Mr. Grumpygroo's head, she smiled, for he looked so very funny.

Grumpygroo thought she was smiling at him, for of course he didn't know what he had on his head, and he was most surprised. He didn't smile back, but went on his way, puzzled to know why the Balloon-Woman should have looked so friendly for the first time in twenty years.

The next person he met was Mr. Sooty, the village sweep. Mr. Sooty loved a joke, and when he saw the lamp-shade perched on old Grumpygroo's head, he grinned very broadly indeed, and showed all his beautiful white teeth.

Mr. Grumpygroo blinked in surprise. The sweep usually called out something rude after him, and certainly he had never smiled at him before. Could it be the fine spring morning that was making people so friendly?

"I shall smile back at the very next person who smiles at me," said Grumpygroo to himself, feeling quite excited. "If people are going to be friendly, I don't mind being nice too."

Round the corner he met Straws the farmer riding on his old horse. As soon as the farmer caught sight of the lamp-shade, he smiled so widely that his mouth almost reached his ears.

And Grumpygroo smiled back! Straws nearly fell off his horse with astonishment, for no one had ever seen such a thing before! He ambled on, lost in surprise, and Grumpygroo went on his way with a funny warm feeling round his heart.

"I've smiled again!" he said to himself. "I've forgotten how nice it was. I hope someone else smiles at me, for I wouldn't mind doing it a second time."

Four little children came running up the street. As soon as they saw Grumpygroo with the yellow lamp-shade on his head, they smiled and laughed in delight.

Grumpygroo was so pleased. He smiled too, and the ice round his heart melted a little bit more. The children laughed merrily and one of them put her hand in his, for she thought Grumpygroo had put the lamp-shade on to amuse her.

Something funny happened inside Grumpygroo. He wanted to sing and dance. He wanted to give pennies away and hug someone. It was lovely to have people so friendly towards him. He put his hand in his pocket, and brought out four bright pennies. He gave one to each child, and they kissed him and ran to the sweet-shop to spend their money, waving and laughing as they went.

Mr. Grumpygroo rubbed his hands in delight. It was lovely to be smiled at and kissed. He would show the people of Tweedle village what a fine, generous person he was, now that they were being so nice to him!

The next person he met was Mr. Crumbs, the baker. Grumpygroo smiled at him before Mr. Crumbs had time to smile first. The baker was so surprised that he nearly dropped the load of new-made cakes he was carrying. Then he saw Grumpygroo's lamp-shade hat, and he gave a deep chuckle. Grumpygroo was delighted to see him so friendly.

"Good morning," he said to Crumbs. "It's a wonderful day, isn't it?"

The baker nodded his head and laughed again.

"Yes," he said; "and that's a wonderful hat you're wearing, Mr. Grumpygroo."

Grumpygroo went on, very much pleased.

"What a nice fellow to admire my old top-hat," he thought. "Dear, dear me, and I always thought the people of Tweedle village were so unpleasant. That just shows how mistaken I can be!"

He smiled at everyone he met, and everyone smiled back, wondering why Grumpygroo wore such a funny thing on his head.

By the time he reached home again, he was quite a different man. He smiled and hummed a little tune, and he even did a little jig when he got into his front garden. He was so happy to think that people had been friendly to him.

"It shows I can't be so grumpy and cross as they thought I was," he said to himself. "Well, well, I'll show them what a fine man I am. I'll give a grand party, and invite everyone in the village to it. Whatever will they say to that!"

He walked into his hall, and was just going to take off his hat when he saw himself in the mirror. He stood and stared in surprise and dismay – whatever *had* he got on his head!

"Oh my, oh my, it's the lamp-shade!" he groaned, and he took it off. "Fancy going out in that! And oh dear! Everyone smiled at the lamp-shade, because it looked so funny – they didn't smile at *me*!"

How upset Grumpygroo was! He sat down in his armchair and thought about it, and after a while he became very much ashamed of himself.

"How dreadful to have to wear a lamp-shade on my head before people will smile at me!" he groaned. "I must be a most unpleasant old man. Well, well! I don't see why I shouldn't have my party. Perhaps the village folk will learn to smile at me for myself if I am nice to them. I'll send out those invitations at once!"

He did – and wasn't everybody surprised!

"Fancy old Grumpygroo giving a party!" they said. "Something must have happened to make him nicer! Do you remember how funny he looked yesterday when he wore that lamp-shade?"

The party was a great success, and soon old Grumpygroo had heaps of friends. Nobody could imagine what had changed the old man and made him so nice, nor could anyone understand why he kept his old yellow lamp-shade so carefully, long after it was dirty and torn.

But Grumpygroo knew why! It had brought him smiles and plenty of friends – but he wasn't going to tell anyone that – not he!

The Boy Who Boasted

SAMMY was always getting into trouble with the other children because he boasted. I expect you know children who boast, and I'm quite sure you don't like them a bit.

"I've got a bigger kite than anyone in the village," Sammy would say. "And it flies higher than anybody else's! Ho, you should just see it!"

Then, when George brought his new engine to school to show everyone, Sammy boasted again.

"Pooh! That's only a clockwork engine. You should see mine at home. It goes by electricity!"

"Don't boast," said George, feeling suddenly that his engine wasn't so nice as he had thought it was.

But Sammy couldn't seem to stop boasting. "I can run faster than any boy at school!" he boasted to his father. "I can do more sums in half an hour than anyone else. I can write better than anyone in my class."

"Well, it's a pity your school reports aren't better then," said his father. "Stop boasting about what you can do, and *do* something for a change. Then I might believe you."

Now Sammy might have gone on boasting for the rest of his life if something hadn't happened. It's a good thing it did happen, because though it's bad enough to hear a child boasting, it's ten times worse to hear a grown-up doing the same thing. I'll tell you what happened.

One day Sammy was going home from school when he picked up a most peculiar pocket-knife. It was bright yellow, with blue ends, and when Sammy opened the blades, he saw that they were made of green steel. He stood and stared at the knife, wondering who had lost it.

And because he was an honest boy, he looked round to see if he could find the owner. Not far off was someone as small as himself and he was hunting everywhere on the ground.

"Hi, boy!" shouted Sammy. "Have you lost a knife, because I've found one?"

The little fellow looked up – and Sammy couldn't quite make him out. He was as small as a boy and yet he looked more like a grown-up. He was dressed a bit strangely, too, in a green tunic and long stockings, and he wore a pointed hat on his head with a bell at the tip.

"Oh," said the little fellow, "have you found my knife? Thank you! My name is Smink. What's yours?"

"Sammy," said Sammy. "That's a funny-looking knife. I've got one at home. It's better than yours – much sharper. It can cut through wood like butter!"

"Oh, mine's sharper than that," said Smink. "It can cut through a tree-trunk like butter!"

"Fibber!" said Sammy. "You're boasting."

"Well, so are you," said Smink. "But I'm telling the truth and you're not. Look!"

And, to Sammy's enormous surprise, Smink went up to a birch tree, drew his knife right through the trunk, and cut the tree in half! Crash! It fell to the ground.

Sammy was startled. "Gracious!" he said. "That knife of yours certainly *is* sharp. But you'll get into trouble if you cut trees down like that."

"I was only showing you," said Smink. He lifted the little tree up again and set it on its trunk. He took a tube of sticky stuff from his pocket and rubbed some on the tree and its trunk. Then it stood upright, looking quite itself again.

"It'll grow all right again," said Smink. "That is Growing-Glue I used. Stronger than any glue you've ever used, I'm sure!"

"Well, at home I've got a tube of glue that will stick all kinds of broken things," said Sammy, beginning to boast again. "It will stick legs on to tables, and backs on to chairs, and . . ."

"Fibber," said Smink. "You haven't any glue strong enough to do that. Now this glue of mine is so strong it would even stick your feet to the ground."

"You're boasting," said Sammy. "I shan't listen to you."

"All right, I'll prove it," said Smink – and quick as lightning, he tipped Sammy over so that he fell to the ground, and then Smink dabbed a little glue on the sole of each shoe. Sammy jumped to his feet in a rage, meaning to slap Smink – but, dear me, the little fellow had spoken the truth – Sammy's feet *were* stuck to the ground. He couldn't move a step.

"Oh, oh, my feet won't move!" he shouted in a temper. "Take your glue away."

"Can't," said Smink with a grin. "You'll have to get out of your shoes and leave them behind."

And that's just what poor Sammy had to do! He slipped his feet out of his shoes and ran at Smink in his socks.

"I'm the strongest boy in my class!" he shouted. "So look out for yourself!"

But Smink was off like the wind. "It won't help you to run away," panted Sammy. "I can run faster than any boy in my school. I'll soon catch you."

"Well, I can run faster than any boy alive!" yelled Smink. And he certainly could. There was no doubt about that at all – he went like the wind. Sammy couldn't possibly catch him. Smink sat down on a grassy bank and let Sammy catch him up that way.

"Now I warn you – don't hit me," said Smink, "because although you may think you can slap harder than anyone in your village, I can smack harder than any boy anywhere. So be careful."

But Sammy wasn't careful! He gave Smink a slap – and Smink at once jumped up and smacked Sammy so hard that he fell to the ground and rolled over three times!

"Oooh!" he said, sitting up. "What hit me then?"

"I did," said Smink. "Don't say I didn't warn you."

"I'll tell my mother and father about you," said Sammy, beginning to cry. "And you'll be sorry then, because my father and mother are big and strong and they will punish you hard."

"Well, my mother and father are big and strong too," said Smink. "There they are, walking over there. Would you like to see what they do to horrid boys like you?"

Sammy looked to where Smink pointed – and to his surprise, saw two very tall, rather fierce-looking people walking through the wood. They were so tall that Sammy half-wondered if they could be giants! He decided at once that he didn't want to have anything to do with them.

"Don't call them," he said hurriedly to Smink. "I can see how big and strong they are without them coming any nearer. Where do you live?"

"In this wood," said Smink. "Where do you?"

"In the village," said Sammy. "And our house is the biggest one there, and it has the best garden too. And we've got a pond. You should just see it."

"I live in a castle," said Smink. "Our garden is so big that we keep fifty gardeners. And our pond is a lake with a steamer on it."

"Oh, you really are a most dreadful fibber," said Sammy, quite shocked.

"I'll slap you again if you call me a fibber," said Smink. "I don't boast like you. What I say is always true. Come with me and I'll show you."

He dragged Sammy off by the arm – and in a few minutes, to Sammy's enormous astonishment, they came to a great wooden gate let into a high wall. Smink pushed it open – and there, set in the most beautiful grounds, was a real, proper castle with towers and all! And working in the garden were so many gardeners that Sammy felt there might even be more than fifty!

"Oooh! There's the lake," he said. "And it really has got a steamer on it. Goodness, aren't you lucky? Have you got a bicycle or a tricycle to ride? I've got a wonderful tricycle. I'm sure it's the best in the world. Its bell rings so loudly that everyone gets out of the way at once."

"I'll show you *my* tricycle," said Smink, and he went to a nearby shed. He opened the door and wheeled out a most marvellous tricycle!

"It's made of gold," said Smink, and he got on it. "Out of the way, boy."

He rode straight at Sammy, ringing the bell – and my word, the noise that bell made! It was like a hundred church bells clanging together at once. Sammy put his hands to his ears and fled out of the way of the swift tricycle.

"Stop ringing the bell!" he cried. "Oh, stop! It's making me deaf."

Smink stopped. He got off the tricycle and grinned. "Do you want to see anything else?" he asked.

"Well, I must be getting home," said Sammy, feeling that he had seen quite enough for one day. "My puppy-dog will be missing me. I bet you haven't got a pup half as nice as mine. Do you know, mine's got a bark that would frighten any burglar at once, and his teeth are so big and sharp. And run – well, you should just see him! He could run you off your feet any day!"

"Well, I've got a puppy, too," said Smink. "And he's got a marvellous bark. And teeth! Gracious, you should see them! They're so sharp that when he took a dislike to the lawn-mower yesterday, he just chewed it all up! And when he runs you can't see his legs, they go so fast!"

"Oh, don't boast," said Sammy, in disgust. But Smink wasn't going to have Sammy saying that. He went to a big yard and opened a gate. He whistled – and out of the kennel there came a simply enormous puppy, gambolling round happily. He barked – and it sounded like the crash of a gun! He growled – and it was like the rumbling of a thunderstorm! He showed his enormous teeth, and Sammy shivered. Goodness, yes – this puppy could chew up a lawn-mower and never notice it!

Sammy began to run. He was afraid of that big puppy. The puppy gambolled after him merrily. Sammy ran faster. The puppy snapped playfully at his ankles. Sammy was simply terrified. He felt certain that the puppy could chew him up just as his own puppy at home had chewed up his father's slipper.

Poor Sammy! He tore home in his socks, and felt the puppy snapping at his heels the whole way. Not until he was indoors and had slammed the door did he feel safe. He lay on the sofa, panting, his feet without any shoes, and his socks all in holes.

He told his mother what had happened, and she found it very difficult to believe. "Well, Sammy," she said, "if it's true, you'll have to remember one thing. Never boast again in case you meet another Smink. See what happens when you do!"

So I don't expect he *will* boast again. I guess Smink had a good laugh about it all, don't you?

The Magic Treacle-Jug

Now once when Miggle the goblin was walking home at night through Goblin Village he saw a light in Mother Tick-Tock's cottage window. He stopped and thought for a moment.

"I think I'll go and peep in," he said to himself. "Mother Tick-Tock's grandfather was a wizard, and it's said that she knows plenty of useful spells. I might see something interesting if I go and peep."

So he crept into the front garden and peeped in at the lighted window. Mother Tick-Tock was there, cutting large slices of bread, one after the other.

"I suppose those are for her children's supper," thought Miggle, counting them. "One, two, three, four, five, six, seven – yes, they are. Goodness me – does she give them just dry bread for their suppers, poor things?"

He watched carefully. He saw Mother Tick-Tock take up a small purple jug and he heard her speak to it.

"Pour me treacle, strong and sweet,
For a very special treat!"

And, to Miggle's surprise, the jug left Mother Tick-Tock's hand, poised itself above a slice of bread, and poured out good, thick, yellow treacle! Then it balanced itself above the next slice and poured more tracle. Then it went to the third slice.

"Good gracious me! How can a little jug like that hold so much treacle!" thought Miggle, in surprise. "Look at it, pouring thickly over one slice after another. What lovely treacle too – oooh, I wish I had some of it!"

Mother Tick-Tock suddenly caught sight of Miggle's face at the window, and, leaving the jug pouring treacle on the last slice of all, she ran to the window, shouting angrily. Miggle disappeared at once and ran home at top speed. He was afraid of Mother Tick-Tock.

But he couldn't forget that wonderful Treacle-Jug. To think of having rich sweet treacle at any time! How lucky Mother Tick-Tock's children were. No wonder he so often saw them about with thick slices of bread and treacle.

Now two days later Miggle made himself a fine pudding. But when he came to taste it he found that he had left out the sugar. Oooh – how horrid it was!

"Now, if only I could borrow that Treacle-Jug!" thought Miggle, longingly.

"I could have treacle all over my pudding and it would be one of the nicest I'd ever had. I wonder if Mother Tick-Tock would lend me the jug."

Just at that very moment Miggle saw someone passing his cottage, and who should it be but Mother Tick-Tock herself, on her way to visit her friend, Mrs. Know-A-Lot. Miggle watched her go down the road, and a small thought uncurled itself in his mind.

"Couldn't I just borrow the Treacle-Jug for a few minutes? Nobody would ever know. And if it's a magic jug, the treacle would never, never come to an end, so it wouldn't matter my having just a very little!"

He sat and thought about it, looking at his sugarless pudding. Then he popped it back into the oven to keep warm, and ran out of the front door very quickly indeed. "I must get that jug before I change my mind!" he thought. "I'll use it to cover my pudding with treacle, then I'll take it straight back. Run, Miggle, run!"

He came to Mother Tick-Tock's cottage. The door was locked, but the window was open just a crack – a big enough crack for a small goblin to put in a bony little arm and reach on to a shelf for a small purple jug! There! He had got it. But how strange – it was quite empty!

"I'd better not go too fast with it, in case I fall and break it," he thought. So he put it under his coat and walked back slowly. He felt very excited indeed.

He stood the purple jug on his table and fetched his pudding from the oven. "Ha, pudding – you're going to taste very nice in a minute!" he said, and set it down in the middle of his table. He picked up the jug and spoke to it solemnly, just as Mother Tick-Tock had.

"Pour me treacle strong and sweet,
For a very special treat!"

said Miggle. The little jug left his hand at once and poised itself over the pudding. It tilted – and to Miggle's great delight a stream of rich golden treacle poured out and fell on his pudding. Miggle's mouth began to water. Ooooh! That pudding was going to taste very very nice!

"There! That's enough, thank you, little Treacle-Jug," said Miggle at last. "Don't pour any more, or the treacle will spill out of the dish."

But the jug took no notice at all. It went on pouring steadily and Miggle saw that the treacle was now dripping over the edges of the pudding dish. "Hey! Didn't you hear what I said!" he cried. "Stop, jug! You'll ruin my tablecloth!"

But the jug didn't stop. It still hung there in the air, treacle pouring from its little spout. Miggle was angry. He snatched at the jug, but it hopped away in the air and went on pouring in another place.

"*Stop*, jug! Don't pour treacle into my armchair!" shouted Miggle. "Oh my

goodness, look what you've done! Emptied treacle all over the seat of my chair and the cushion! Come away from there!"

He snatched at the jug again, but it wouldn't let itself be caught. It got away from his grabbing hand just in time and hung itself up in the air just above the wash-tub, which was full of Miggle's dirty clothes, soaking in the suds there.

"Hey!" cried Miggle in alarm. "Not over my washing, for goodness' sake! Stop, I say! Don't you see what you're doing? You're not supposed to pour treacle over chairs and wash-tubs, only over puddings and pies. Oh, you mischievous jug! Wait till I get you! I'll break you in half!"

He snatched at the jug again, but it swung away in the air and this time hung itself over his nice new rug.

Trickle, trickle, trickle – the rich, sticky treacle poured down steadily over the rug, and poor Miggle tried to pull it away. But he soon found himself standing in treacle, for it spread gradually over the floor.

Then Miggle began to feel very alarmed indeed. What was he to do with this mad Treacle-Jug? He simply MUST stop it somehow.

"Ah – I've an idea!" thought Miggle. "Where's my fishing-net? I'll get that and catch the jug in it. Then I'll smash it to bits on the ground. Oh, this treacle! How I hate walking in it! It's just like glue!"

He made his way to the corner where he kept his net and took hold of it. At once the Treacle-Jug swung itself over to him and poured treacle down on his head and face. How horrible! How sticky! Miggle was so angry that he shouted at the top of his voice.

"I'll smash you! I'll break you into a hundred pieces!" He swung the fishing-net at the jug and almost caught it. It seemed frightened and swung away out of the door and up the stairs, pouring treacle all the way. Miggle sat down and cried bitterly. Whatever was he to do?

Soon he heard a curious glug-glug noise, and he looked up in alarm. A river of treacle was flowing slowly down the stairs! It flowed through the kitchen and out of the door, down the path and into the street. People passing by were quite astonished.

Mother Tick-Tock, coming back from visiting her friend, was astonished too. But she knew in a trice what had happened.

"Miggle's borrowed my Treacle-Jug!" she said. "I saw him peeping through the window when I used it the other night. The mean, thieving little fellow!"

Miggle saw Mother Tick-Tock and waded out through the treacle river to his front gate, crying, "Please, Mother Tick-Tock, I'm sorry. I can't make the jug stop pouring. Is there a spell to stop it as well as to start it?"

"Of course there is," said Mother Tick-Tock. "It's just as well to know *both* spells if you steal something like a Treacle-Jug, Miggle. Well, you can keep the jug if you like. I've a much bigger one I can use. How tired of treacle you must be, Miggle!"

"Oh, Mother Tick-Tock, please, please take your jug away," begged Miggle, kneeling down in the treacle. "I'll do anything you say, if you only will!"

"Very well. If you come and dig my garden for me all the year round and keep it nice, I'll stop the jug from pouring, and take it back," said Mother Tick-Tock. Miggle groaned. He did so hate gardening!

"I'll come," he said. "I don't want to, but I will."

"If you don't, I'll send the jug to pour over your head," said Mother Tick-Tock, and everyone laughed. She called loudly, "Treacle-Jug, come here!"

The little purple jug sailed out of a bedroom window and hung over Miggle's head. He dodged away at once. Mother Tick-Tock chanted loudly,

"Be empty, jug, and take yourself
Back to your place upon my shelf!"

And – hey presto – the Treacle-Jug became quite empty, turned itself upside-down to show Mother Tick-Tock that it had obeyed her, and then flew swiftly through the air on the way to her cottage. Mother Tick-Tock knew she would find it standing quietly in its place on her kitchen-shelf.

"Well, good-bye, Miggle," she said. "You've quite a lot of cleaning up to do, haven't you? Somehow I don't think you'll want to eat treacle again in a hurry!"

She was right. Poor old Miggle can't even *see* a treacle-tin now without running for miles! And I'm not a bit surprised at that!

"Tell Me My Name!"

THE Hoppetty Gnome lived in a little cottage all by himself. He kept no dog and no cat, but outside in the garden lived a fat, freckled thrush who sang to Hoppetty each morning and evening to thank him for the crumbs he put out.

Hoppetty was very fond of this thrush. She was a pretty bird, and the songs she sang were very lovely.

"The sky is blue, blue!
And all day through, through,
I sing to you, you!"

That was the thrush's favourite song, and Hoppetty knew it by heart.

Now one day a dreadful thing happened. Hoppetty was walking through the wood, going home after his shopping, when out pounced a big goblin and caught hold of him. He put little Hoppetty into a sack and ran off with the struggling gnome over hill and meadow until he came to the tall hill on the top of which he lived. Then he emptied Hoppetty out of his sack, and told him he was to be his cook.

"I am very fond of cakes with jam inside," said the grinning goblin, "and I love chocolate fingers sprinkled with nuts. I have heard that you are a clever cake-maker. Make me these things."

Poor Hoppetty! How he had to work! The goblin really had a most enormous appetite, and as he ate nothing but jam cakes and chocolate fingers, Hoppetty was busy all day long at the oven, baking, baking. He was always hot and always tired. He wondered and wondered who this strange goblin was, and one day he asked him.

"Who are you, Master?" he said.

"Oho! Wouldn't you like to know?" said the goblin, putting six chocolate fingers into his mouth at once. "Well, Hoppetty, if you could guess my name, I'd let you go. But you never will!"

Hoppetty sighed. He was sure he never *would* guess the goblin's name. Goblins had such strange names. Nobody ever came to the house, no letters were pushed through the letter-box, and Hoppetty was never allowed to go out. So how could he possibly find out the goblin's name? He tried a few guesses.

"Is your name Thingumebob?"

"Ho, ho, ho! No, no, no!"

"Is it Mankypetoddle?"

"Ho, ho, ho! No, no, no!"

"Well, is it Tiddleywinks?"

"Ho, ho, ho! No, no, no!"

Then Hoppetty sighed and set to work to make more jam cakes, for the goblin had eaten twenty-two for breakfast, and the larder was getting empty.

The goblin went out and banged the door. He locked it too, and went down the path. Hoppetty knew he couldn't get out. He had tried before. The windows opened two inches, and no more. The door he couldn't open at all. He was indeed a prisoner. He sighed again and set to work quickly.

And then he heard something that made his heart leap. It was a bird singing sweetly.

"The sky is blue, blue!
And all day through, through,
I sing to you, you!"

It was his thrush! Hoppetty rushed to the window and looked out of the open crack. There was the pretty freckled bird, sitting in a nearby tree.

"Thrush!" cried Hoppetty. "I'm here! Oh, you dear creature, have you been going about singing and looking for me? Did you miss your crumbs? I'm a prisoner here. I can only get away if I find out the name of the goblin who keeps me here."

Just then the goblin came back, and the gnome rushed to his baking once more. The thrush sang sweetly outside for a few minutes and then flew away.

The bird was unhappy. It loved little Hoppetty. The gnome had been so kind to her, and had loved her singing so very much. If only the thrush could find out the name of the goblin. But how?

The bird made up her mind to watch the goblin and see where he went. So the next day she followed him when he left the cottage, flying from tree to tree as the goblin went on his way. At last he came to another cottage, and, to the thrush's surprise, the door was opened by a black cat with bright green eyes.

"A witch cat!" thought the thrush. "I wonder if she knows the goblin's name. I dare not ask her, for if I go too near she will spring at me."

The goblin stayed a little while and then went away. The thrush was about to follow, when the cat brought out a spinning-wheel and set it in the sunshine by the door. She sat down and began to spin her wool.

And as she spung, she sang a strange song.

"First of eel, and second of hen,
And after that the fourth of wren,
Third of lean and first of meat,
Second of leg and third of feet.
Fifth of strong and second of pail,
Fourth of hammer and third of nail.
Sixth of button and third of coat,
First of me and second of boat.
When you've played this curious game,
You may perchance have found his name!"

The cat sang this over and over again, and the thrush listened hard. Soon she knew it by heart and at once flew off to the goblin's cottage. She put her head on one side and looked in at the window. Hoppetty was setting the table for the goblin and was talking to him.

"Is your name Twisty-tail?"

"Ho, ho, ho! No, no, no!" roared the goblin.

"Well, is it Twisty-nose?"

"Ho, ho, ho! No, no, no! And don't you be rude!" snapped the goblin.

"Well, is it Pointed-ears?" asked poor Hoppetty.

"Ho, ho, ho! No, no, no! Give me some more jam cakes!" ordered the goblin.

The next day the thrush waited until the goblin had gone out, and then she began to sing sweetly.

Hoppetty knew that it was his own thrush singing, and he went to the window and listened – but what a peculiar song the bird was whistling! The thrush sang the cat's song over and over again – and suddenly Hoppetty guessed that it was trying to tell him how to find the goblin's name. He frowned and thought hard. Yes – he thought he could!

He fetched a pencil and a piece of paper and sat down. The thrush flew to the window-sill and sang the song slowly. Hoppetty put down the words and then he began to work out the puzzle in great excitement.

"The first of eel – that's E. The second of hen – that's E too. The fourth of wren – that's N. The third of lean – A. The first of meat – M. Second of leg – another E. Third of feet – E again! Fifth of strong, that's N. Second of pail – A. Fourth of hammer – M. Third of nail – I. Sixth of button – N. Third of coat – A. First of me – M, and second of coat – O! Now what do all these letters spell?"

He wrote the letters out in a word, and looked at it – EENA-MEENA-MINA-MO!

"So that's the goblin's name!" cried the gnome in excitement. "Oh, I would never, never have thought of that!"

The thrush flew off in a hurry, for she heard the goblin returning. He strode into his cottage and scowled when he saw the gnome sitting down writing instead of baking.

"What's all this?" he roared.

"Is your name Tabby-cat?" asked the gnome, with a grin.

"Ho, ho, ho! No, no, no!" cried the goblin. "Get to your work."

"Is it – is it – Wibbly-Wobbly?" asked the gnome, pretending to be frightened.

"Ho, ho, ho! No, no, no!" shouted the goblin in a rage. "Where are my jam cakes?"

"Is it – can it be – EENA-MEENA-MINA-MO?" cried the gnome suddenly.

The goblin stared at Hoppetty and turned pale. "How do you know that?" he asked, in a frightened whisper. "No one knows it! No one! Now you have found out my secret name! Oh! Oh! Go, you horrid creature! I am afraid of you! What will you find out next?"

He flung the door wide open, and Hoppetty ran out gladly, shouting:

"Eena, Meena, Mina, Mo,
Catch a goblin by his toe;
If he squeals, let him go,
Eena, Meena, Mina, Mo!"

He skipped all the way home – and there, sitting on his garden gate, was his friend the thrush. You can guess that Hoppetty gave her a fine meal of crumbs, and told her all about how angry and frightened the goblin was!

"I shall bake you a cake for yourself every time I have a baking day," he promised. And he did – but, as you can guess, he never again made a jam cake or a chocolate finger!

A Shock for Lucy Ann!

Lucy Ann was a perfect nuisance. She was always putting her nose into other people's business, and interfering in other people's affairs.

"Oh, go away, Lucy Ann!" the children said, when she tried to show them how much better it would be to do things her way and not theirs. "You are always interfering!"

"Oh, run away, Lucy Ann!" her mother would say, when Lucy Ann came poking round, telling her mother that this corner was not dusted, and that picture was hanging all crooked. "I don't need you to come poking your nose everywhere! I can see dusty corners and crooked pictures for myself!"

"Oh, Lucy Ann, please go home!" said Mrs. Brown, who lived down the road. "I don't need *you* to tell me that my garden needs weeding, and that my roses need watering. You are always putting your nose into things that are no business of yours. Go away!"

Lucy Ann frowned and went away. But she didn't stop putting her nose into everything. She made herself such a little nuisance that no one wanted her with them.

One day, as she was coming home from school, she went across the fields. As she came near to the stile, she heard voices talking, and she looked about to see where they came from. To her surprise she saw four little men sitting under the hedge, making daisy chains. But they were not making them in the way that Lucy Ann made them! Instead of stringing the stalks together, they were threading the daisies through their heads.

"Oh!" said Lucy Ann, poking her nose into their play at once. "That's wrong! You shouldn't thread daisies that way! You want to do them like this!"

She snatched the daisies out of the hands of the surprised little men, and began to make holes through their stalks with a pin. The men jumped to their feet in anger – and then Lucy Ann saw that they were brownies. She stared at them, for she had never seen brownies before.

"You nasty, interfering little girl, poking your nose into our affairs!" cried one. "Your nose wants seeing to – it's much too sharp!"

"Let's make it sharper still, so that when she goes about interfering and putting her nose where it isn't wanted, she'll always know!" cried the smallest brownie. He reached out his hand and smacked Lucy Ann sharply on the nose.

"When you poke yourself here,
And poke yourself there,
Just grow longer and sharper
And make people stare!"

cried the brownie at the top of his voice.

"Oh!" cried Lucy Ann in a rage, for the slap hurt her. She was just going to slap the brownie back when there came a puff of smoke from somewhere that hid the four little men – and when the smoke cleared away, the brownies had vanished.

Lucy Ann went home, very angry. Silly little men! She had only tried to show them the right way to make a daisy chain.

Just as she was nearly home she saw two boys she knew, playing marbles on the pavement. She stopped to watch.

"Oh, you silly!" she said to one. "You will never win if you play like that. This is what you should do!"

As she was speaking, a curious thing happened. Her nose grew very long indeed and very sharp. It poked itself among the marbles!

"Look! Look!" screamed the two boys, in fright. "Look at Lucy Ann's nose! It's like an elephant's trunk!"

Lucy Ann shrieked too. It was dreadful to feel her nose waving about like that! She ran home crying loudly. But by the time she was indoors her nose had gone back to its right size again, and her mother laughed at her when Lucy Ann told her what had happened.

But she didn't laugh when she saw it happen again! And it soon did. It was when Lucy Ann's mother was busy reading a letter. Lucy Ann came and peeped to see what was in the letter, for she simply couldn't keep out of anything!

"Who's it from?" she said – and, dear me, just as she said that her nose shot out again, long and sharp and waving, and patted itself on to the letter.

Lucy Ann's mother gave a shriek. "Oh!" she cried, "how dreadful you look, Lucy Ann! Whatever has happened to your nose?"

Lucy Ann began to cry again. She told her mother about the brownies, and her mother nodded and frowned.

"Yes, you offended the little folk," she said, "and they punished you. Now your nose will always grow long and sharp whenever you poke it where it isn't wanted. Oh, Lucy Ann, what a dreadful, dreadful thing! You had better come with me to old Mother Eleanor's. She knows a bit about magic and may put it right for you."

So, crying bitterly, Lucy Ann went to Mother Eleanor's with her mother. But when Mother Eleanor heard what had happened, she laughed.

"I *could* take the spell out of her nose in a jiffy!" she said. "But I shan't!"

"Oh, but what will poor Lucy Ann do!" cried her mother.

"Do?" said Mother Eleanor. "Why, keep it right herself, of course! It only grows long and sharp when she pokes it where it isn't wanted, doesn't it? Well, if she stops poking her nose into everything it won't grow long and wave about like that!"

Lucy Ann went home with her mother, and thought hard. Her nose would never be cured – unless she cured it herself! She had better try. She wouldn't interfere with any one. She would be sensible and say nothing, even when she badly wanted to poke her nose in somewhere!

Poor Lucy Ann! It wasn't so easy as she thought! Every day her nose shot out long and sharp, and every day people screamed at her or laughed loudly. But at last she tried so hard that a whole week went by and her nose stayed its right size and shape. And then she forgot again and out it shot, long and sharp, sticking itself here and there!

Lucy Ann was ashamed. She tried hard again – and, do you know, she hasn't let her nose grow long for more than a year now! She has gone to a new school, where the children don't know anything about the spell in her nose. I do hope she doesn't poke it where it isn't wanted again – because those children *will* be surprised to see what happens, won't they?

The Snoozy Gnome

HAVE you heard of the Snoozy Gnome? His real name was Tippit, but he was always called Snoozy. He was the sleepiest, yawniest fellow that ever lived! He could go to sleep at any time – even whilst running to catch a bus!

Now one day Snoozy's village was tremendously excited. The Prince of Heyho was coming for the day, and so the gnomes decided to give a fancy dress party in his honour.

"It shall be at five o'clock in the afternoon, so that even the tiniest gnome can come," said Mister Big-Nose, the chief gnome. "Now all go home, please, and make some really good fancy dresses for the party!"

Snoozy went home and sat down to think. "I shall be a bear!" he decided excitedly. "I can wear my bearskin rug, and pull the head right over my head. I will pin it tightly round me – and dear me, how astonished everyone will be! That will be a fine fancy dress!"

When the day came, Snoozy took up his bearskin rug and tried it on his back. He crawled about with the bear-head over his head, and the rug over his back. He really looked fine – just like a real bear!

"It's a bit big round my neck," thought Snoozy. "I must alter that. Let me see – what is the time? Oh, only two o'clock. I've got heaps of time till five."

He got out a big needle and a strong thread and sat down to make the neck of the bearskin a little smaller. It was a hot afternoon and Snoozy rested his head against a soft cushion. He was very comfortable.

"Aaaaaah!" he yawned. "My goodness, I'd like a nap. I do feel sleepy!"

He looked at the clock again. "I think I'd have time just for ten minutes' snooze," he decided. "Then I shall be all fresh for the party!"

So he lay back and fell asleep. The time went on – three o'clock, four o'clock, five o'clock! And still Snoozy slept on! He dreamed pleasant dreams. He was as warm as toast, and his armchair was very comfortable. Oh, what a lovely snooze!

Time went on – six o'clock, seven o'clock, eight o'clock, nine o'clock. Snoozy, aren't you *ever* going to wake up? The party is over – everyone has gone home – and Mister Big-Nose is wondering why Snoozy didn't go to the party like everyone else!

Ten o'clock, eleven o'clock, midnight! The kitchen fire went out, and everywhere was quite dark and silent. Snoozy slept on, dreaming pleasantly. The clock ticked out the minutes in the darkness – but when the hands reached five minutes past four in the early morning, the clock stopped. It had to be wound up every night and as Snoozy had been asleep the evening before, it hadn't been wound up as usual.

After that there was no more ticking, and no more chiming. But the time went on – five o'clock, six o'clock, seven o'clock, eight o'clock! The sun was up, and most of the folk of the village. And at last Snoozy stirred in his armchair and stretched out his arms. He yawned widely – and opened his eyes. He looked round the room – and then he remembered the fancy dress party! My goodness!

"What's the time?" said Snoozy, and looked at the clock. "Five minutes past four! Gracious goodness, and the party is at five! I must hurry. I have had a longer snooze than I meant to have. Dear, dear, now I *shall* have to rush!"

You see, Snoozy hadn't any idea at all that he had slept all the night through. He simply thought he had slept till five minutes past four the day before – and he thought it was yesterday, not to-day! Poor old Snoozy! He didn't think of looking at the sun to see whereabouts in the sky it was, for, like most sleepy-headed people, he was rather stupid – and though the sun shone in at the wrong window, he still thought it was the afternoon!

"I shan't have time to alter the bearskin now," said Snoozy to himself. "Can't be bothered! My, how hungry I am! I shall eat quite twenty cakes at the party, and I believe I could manage two or three jellies, and as for sausage-rolls, aha, give me fifteen of those, and you won't see them again!"

He put on the bearskin rug and pinned it tightly all round him. Then he pulled the bear-head over his own head, and pinned it well round his neck. He could hardly breathe, but he didn't mind. He was pleased to think he had such a fine fancy dress!

"Now, off we go!" said Snoozy and, crawling on all fours, he went out of his front door and down the street. As he went, he growled, because he thought that would make people look round and say: "Oh, look! Here's someone in a wonderful fancy dress!"

But the party was over long ago – and the folk of the village were hurrying to do their morning shopping. When they saw the life-like bear walking down the street, growling, they were frightened.

"Oh, oh!" they cried. "Look at that monster! He came out of Snoozy's house – he must have eaten him! Run, run!"

"Get a gun and shoot him!" cried Mister Big-Nose, meeting the bear round a corner, and getting the fright of his life.

Now Snoozy could NOT understand all this. So he stood up on his hind paws and shouted – or tried to shout through the bear-head: "I'm going to the party. Don't be frightened of me!"

But all that came out of the bear-head was something that sounded like: "Ah-wah-wah-wah-wah-wah-wah! Wah-wah-wah-wah-wah-wah!" It was really very difficult to speak with a big bear-head over his face, and Snoozy tried his best to talk clearly.

"Oh! It's growling at us! It's a *fierce* bear!" shouted everyone in terror. "Listen to it jabbering!"

Poor Snoozy was now quite puzzled. How stupid people were! Couldn't they even *guess* that it was a fancy dress? He shouted again, trying to say: "I tell you, I'm going to the fancy dress party! Don't you UNDERSTAND?"

But all that came out was something like: "Ah-who-wah, sh-wsh-wah-woo-wah-woowoowoo-wah! Wah-woo – YAH-HAY-YAH!"

"Oh! It's getting fiercer!" yelled the frightened people. "Mister Big-Nose, fetch a gun! Oh, get a spear! Oh, where's a great big stick to knock it on the head! It'll eat us!"

Snoozy was now quite frightened. A gun! A spear! A stick to knock him on the head! Really, was everyone quite mad? Wasn't he telling them he was going to the party?

"I think I'd better go to the Town Hall, where the party is to be held, and then when people see me going up the steps, they will know I'm just someone in fancy dress," said Snoozy to himself. So he dropped down on all fours again and padded off to the Town Hall. Behind him came crowds of people, talking, pointing, and all ready to run away at once if the bear so much as turned his head.

But he didn't. He went right on to the Town Hall. He padded up the steps and into the big hall where three gnomes were busily sweeping up all the mess from the party the day before.

Snoozy stopped and looked in astonishment. "*Where* was the party?" he wondered. "No tea – no balloons – no people there – no nothing!"

He spoke to the three servants, who had been so busy with their work that they hadn't noticed the bear padding in. Snoozy said: "Where is the PARTY?"

But all the three servants heard was: "Wah-wah-wah-wah."

"Ooooooh!" they screeched in fright, when they saw the bear. "Oooooh! A wild bear! Growling at us! Chase him out, chase him out!"

So, to Snoozy's great surprise and anger, the three little gnomes rushed at him with big brooms and swept him out of the Town Hall! Yes, they really did, and it was very brave of them for they really and truly thought he was a wild bear from the woods.

"Don't! Don't!" yelled poor Snoozy. But as it sounded like "Woof! Woof!" it didn't help him much.

Bump, bumpity, bump-bump! Down the steps of the Town Hall went Snoozy, right to the very bottom. The three gnomes ran down after him and swept him into a very large puddle.

Snoozy was terribly upset. He sat in the puddle and cried loudly: "Boo-hoo-hoo! Boo-hoo-hoo!"

And this time the noise he made was really like someone weeping, and all the villagers stopped and looked at one another.

"The bear is crying!" they said. "The bear is crying! Poor thing! Perhaps he has come with a message to someone. Ask him, Big-Nose!"

So Mister Big-Nose stepped forward and spoke to the bear. "Why have you come?" he said. "Do you want to speak to someone?"

"No," said Snoozy, and it sounded like "Woof!"

Big-Nose shook his head. "We can't understand what you say," he said.

Just then a small, sharp-eyed gnome gave a shout and pointed to the bear's neck. "He's got a safety-pin there!" he cried. "Do you think it is hurting him?"

"Where?" said Big-Nose, astonished. When he saw the safety-pin, he was very sorry for the bear. "Someone has put the pin there," he said. "Poor thing! Perhaps he came to ask us to take it out."

He undid the pin – and to his enormous surprise, the bear's head dropped sideways, and out of it came – Snoozy's own head, very hot, very rumpled, and with tears pouring down his cheeks!

"SNOOZY! It's SNOOZY!" cried everyone in the greatest astonishment. "What *are* you doing in a bearskin, Snoozy?"

"I c-c-came to the fancy dress p-p-party!" wept Snoozy. "But I couldn't find it."

"But that was *yesterday*, Snoozy!" said Big-Nose. "We wondered why you didn't come."

"Yesterday!" said Snoozy. "But I thought it was to be on Wednesday, not Tuesday."

"To-day is Thursday," said Big-Nose. "What *have* you been doing, Snoozy? Have you been asleep or something – and slept all round the clock? This is Thursday morning. What did you think it was?"

"Why, I thought it was Wednesday afternoon! And I came out dressed in my bearskin rug to go to the party. And now I've missed the party – and got swept down the steps – and I'm bruised all over! Oh, why did I take that snooze! I must have slept all the afternoon and all the night – and my clock stopped at five past four, and I thought that was the real time!"

Everyone began to laugh. It was really such a joke. "Snoozy came to the party the day after!" said one gnome to another. "Poor old Snoozy! What *will* he do next! And he was swept down the steps, too! Ho, ho! Perhaps he won't be quite so snoozy next time!"

Snoozy went home, carrying the bearskin over his shoulder. He was very unhappy. He got himself some bread and jam, for he was very hungry, and then he sat down to eat it. But so many tears ran down his nose into the jam that they made it taste quite salty, and he didn't enjoy his breakfast at all.

"That's the last time I snooze!" said the gnome. "Never again!"

But it takes more than one lesson to cure a snoozer. Before a week was out, Snoozy was napping again – what a sleepy-head he is!

You Can't Trick Brer Rabbit!

IT HAPPENED once that Brer Fox thought of a good way to catch Brer Rabbit for his dinner. He waited until he saw Brer Rabbit coming down the lane, and then he started limping as if one of his legs was badly hurt.

"Ooh my, ooh my!" he groaned, pretending that he didn't see Brer Rabbit. "I'm sure I shan't get home! My leg's broken, that's certain!"

He suddenly fell down on the ground, and lay there making a great hullabaloo. Brer Rabbit stopped a little way behind him in surprise.

"What's the matter, Brer Fox?" he asked.

"I've just broken my leg," said Brer Fox. "You come and help me home, Brer Rabbit, there's a good fellow. Give me your arm, for I can't walk alone. You mustn't leave me here like this, for I'd die. I can't walk another step!"

But Brer Rabbit wasn't easily tricked. "You wait there, Brer Fox," he said. "I'll get help for you."

"But I'll die before you bring help," said Brer Fox, making a great moaning noise again. "You come along and help me now, Brer Rabbit."

"I'll go and get you something to eat, first," said Brer Rabbit. "That will get your strength up so's you'll be able to walk with me."

"That's kind of you, Brer Rabbit," said Brer Fox. So off went Brer Rabbit. Nearby was Brer Bear's house, and Brer Rabbit knew he had been baking a meat-pie that day. He saw that Brer Bear had put it on the window-sill to cool. He snatched it up and ran off to Brer Fox with it.

"Here you are, Brer Fox," he said. "You eat that up and you'll feel better. I'll be back in two shakes of a duck's tail to help you home."

Brer Fox took the pie greedily and began to gobble it up. Brer Rabbit rushed back to Brer Bear's house and banged on the door, crying, "Heyo, Brer Bear! Have you lost a fine meat-pie? There's old Brer Fox a-sitting down the lane, and he's gobbling up a pie as fast as he can!"

Brer Bear went to the window-sill to see if his pie was there, and when he saw it was gone, he shouted in a fearful rage.

"Stars and moon! It's gone. I'll bite Brer Fox's head off for that!"

Off he ran out into the lane, grunting and growling most fearsomely. "Oy, oy, yi, yi, where's Brer Fox? I'll bite his head off! I'll gobble his tail! I'll cook his whiskers! Where's my meat-pie?"

As soon as Brer Fox heard this awful noise and saw Brer Bear pounding down the lane he turned pale with fright. He threw the pie into the hedge and leapt to his feet.

"You mind your broken leg, Brer Fox!" yelled Brer Rabbit, laughing fit to kill himself. "You mind that broken leg!"

But Brer Fox didn't wait to think of his leg. No, it had mended itself all in a hurry, and you couldn't see him for dust! As for old Brer Rabbit, he took the pie out of the hedge and sat down to enjoy it. It's a pity to waste anything, isn't it?

Prince Rollo's Kite

THERE was once a magician who wanted gold. He was not clever at magic, and he made very little money at selling spells, for he didn't make them very well.

But he wanted to be rich, very rich. He wanted to have sacks of gold in his cellar, and hundreds of servants round him. He wanted to wear rich silver and gold cloaks, and to have a carriage drawn by twenty black horses.

"I shall have to think of some clever idea," he thought, "that will bring me plenty of money without too much hard work."

He knew that was a bad way to get money. Nothing but good work should bring good money, but Griffin was lazy and he didn't like hard work. So he sat and thought for a long time.

But he couldn't think of anything. "I'll put on my tall hat and my grand flowing cloak, and go out walking in the field," he thought at last. "Maybe an idea will come to me then."

So out he went. He walked near the castle grounds, where the Prince and Princess of High-Up lived. Great fields lay round the castle, and in one of the fields was a small boy.

Griffin watched him. He was trying to fly a kite. His kite was yellow, and had a short tail of screwed-up papers. Griffin knew it was too short. The kite would never fly with such a short tail. It would simply dive down all the time.

Then he suddenly saw that the small boy was the little Prince Rollo, son of the rich Prince and Princess of High-Up. What was he doing there in the fields alone? He always had some servant with him to guard him – but to-day he was quite alone.

It was then that Griffin's idea came to him. "Of course," he thought, "if only I could capture the little prince and hide him away somewhere, the Prince and Princess would offer a very large sum of money for him! How marvellous! I should get my cellars full of gold without doing a stroke of work."

He looked about cautiously and saw that there were no servants about at all. The little prince was quite alone. Griffin went up to him, smiling a kind smile.

"Little Prince Rollo," he said, "your kite hasn't a long enough tail! That's why it won't fly on this windy day. Poor child, it's disappointing for you!"

"I'll go back to the castle and make a longer tail," said Prince Rollo, not at all liking the look of the tall magician.

"Oh, don't bother to do that," said the magician. "Come with me. My house is just over there, look – and I will make you a tail with magic in it for your kite. Then it will fly marvellously, and tug at the string like a live thing."

"I should like that," said Rollo. "All right, I'll come with you for a few minutes, if you'll make a new tail. I mustn't be long, though, because no one knows I have stolen out by myself to fly my kite, and I'm sure to be missed soon."

"Hurry, then!" said Griffin. "Look, come under my cloak and walk there – then if we meet anyone no one will know where you are."

So Rollo was wrapped in the big flowing cloak and whisked off to the magician's house without anyone knowing. But once there, Griffin became very different. He locked the doors and put the shutters over the windows. "Why do you do that?" asked Rollo, in alarm.

"Because you are my little prisoner now!" said Griffin. "Aha! I'll get plenty of money for you from your anxious father and mother."

"What a hateful trick!" cried Rollo. "I'll not let you do that! I'll fight you!"

He dropped his kite and rushed at Griffin. But the magician muttered a few magic words and disappeared into thin air. Rollo couldn't fight someone he couldn't see.

"Coward!" he called. "You're a coward! Come and fight! I'm smaller than you are. You're afraid!"

Griffin boxed Rollo's ears hard. It was strange to feel hands he couldn't see. Rollo knew then that he couldn't hope to fight the magician with his hands. He must fight him with his brain! "All right," said the boy. "You win! But I warn you – if you treat me badly it will be worse for you afterwards! Treat me well, and my parents will proabably be so glad that they will not try to catch you afterwards."

"You behave yourself and I'll treat you all right," said Griffin. "And don't think you can possibly escape, because you can't. To-night I shall spirit you away to a lonely hill, where I know of a tiny cottage. No one lives near it for miles."

Rollo certainly couldn't escape that day. He was locked in the one little room, whose windows were shuttered fast. There was no way out at all. He sat there gloomily, looking at his kite, and wishing he hadn't slipped out to fly it by himself.

That night the magician took him away. He spirited him off whilst he slept, so the little prince had no idea how Griffin had taken him. He thought he must have used some very powerful magic.

He awoke next morning in a small cottage set on the top of a windy hillside, sheltered by pine-trees at the back. He ran to the window. All round lay desolate country and thick woods. Not a house was to be seen!

"I should get lost if I tried to escape from here," he thought. "I wouldn't know which way to go."

Griffin seemed to read his thoughts. "Yes – it would indeed be foolish to try and escape from here," he said. "You would lose your way and starve. Better to stay here with me until your parents pay me your ransom in sacks of gold – then I will take you back in safety."

"You're a wicked fellow," said Rollo. "Wickedness is always punished in the end, always."

"Pooh," said Griffin. "Don't you believe it."

"Well, I do believe it," said Rollo. "And you'll believe it, too, some day. You'll be caught, magician, I know you will! You won't get your sacks of gold!"

But Griffin felt certain that he would, and he sent a pigeon off that very day with a message to the Prince and Princess of High-Up, to tell them that he was holding the boy Rollo for ransom. He rubbed his hands with glee as he watched the pigeon fly off into the sky, with the message tied round one of its legs.

He fed the little prince well, and gave him a warm and comfortable bed. But the boy was bored. "There's nothing for me to *do*!" he said. "Let me go and fly my kite on the hill. You brought it here with me, and I'd like to fly it."

"Very well. You can," said Griffin. "I'll watch from the window to make sure you don't try any silly tricks and run away."

Rollo took his kite out. But, just as before, it wouldn't fly properly. As soon as he got it up into the wind it dived down in circles to the ground again. It was very disappointing.

Griffin called to him: "It wants a longer tail. I told you that before."

Rollo ran in. "Well – can I make a longer tail?" he asked. "I'd like that. A really long one. Have you got any paper?"

The magician had some sheets of white paper. He gave them to Rollo.

"You tear each one in half and fold it and then tie it by the middle of the fold to the tail-string," he said. "Your kite will fly beautifully then."

Griffin didn't help Rollo. He went out into the little kitchen to use a few spells to prepare a good dinner. He knew how to conjure up pies and puddings, and that was very useful indeed.

The wind slammed the door shut. Rollo was alone. He began to tear the paper into halves. Then, with a quick glance to make sure the door was still shut, he took a pencil from his pocket. He wrote a message on the first piece of paper and then folded it and tied it firmly to the bit of string that was the kite's tail.

He did the same with the second bit and the third bit. What did he write? He wrote: "I am the Prince Rollo. I have been captured by Griffin, the magician. I am in a small cottage on a faraway hill, with lonely country all round. There are pine-trees behind the cottage. Far, far away I can see the top of another hill, shaped like four teeth at the top. Please rescue me. Rollo."

He wrote each sentence on a different bit of paper, and tied it firmly to the tail-string. He made a very long tail indeed.

Then he sat and looked at his kite. "Suppose I set you free and you fly for miles, and someone finds you where you fall – how will they know that they must undo the papers that make your tail?" he thought. Then he took his pencil and scribbled in big letters over the kite itself. "Look well at my *beautiful* tail!"

Just as he had finished the magician came in. "Ah!" he said, "that is a better tail. Now your kite should fly beautifully. I will come and watch. But what is this you have scribbled on the kite?"

"I've put 'Look well at my *beautiful* tail!'" said Rollo, "so that all the birds the kite meets will admire it!"

"What a baby you are!" said Griffin, scornfully. "As if the birds will know or care! Come along – we'll go and fly it now and then have our meal."

They went out into the strong wind. Rollo let the kite up into the air at once. Ah, now indeed it flew well with its grand new tail to keep it steady. Higher it flew and higher and the wind pulled more and more strongly!

Rollo had a big ball of string, and he unravelled it fast. The ball grew smaller and smaller – it came to the very end!

"Hold it, hold it, or you'll lose your kite!" cried Griffin. The wind gave an extra strong pull – and took the end of the string from Rollo's fingers! Then away flew the kite into the sky, free and happy.

"You silly boy! Why didn't you hold on?" said the magician. Rollo pretended to burst into tears. He buried his face in his hands and howled loudly.

"Well, it was your own fault," said the magician. "Now your kite will fly for miles, and then, when the wind drops, it will drop too. Down to the ground it will go and some other boy will find it."

But it wasn't a boy who found the kite the next day, miles and miles away from Rollo. It was a little girl called Sukie. The kite fell into the garden, and she saw it there when she went out to play.

"Oh, what a lovely kite!" she said, and she ran to it. She stared at its face, and saw something written there.

"Look well as my *beautiful* tail!" she read. She looked at the kite's tail. It didn't seem at all beautiful to her. It was just made of strips of folded white paper.

All the same she felt that there must be some meaning in the message. She made up her mind to untie one of the tail-strips, and to her enormous surprise she read:

"I am the Prince Rollo!"

Well, everyone knew by now that the little prince had been captured, and Sukie knew at once what the message meant. With trembling hands she undid each paper-strip and soon she knew the whole story. She flew indoors to her mother to tell her.

Then what a to-do there was! The police were told, the Prince and Princess of High-up were sent for, soldiers galloped here and there, and all the people began to talk about the message the kite had brought.

"It will be easy to find the Prince," said the soldiers. "We know the hill with four teeth-like rocks at the top. From there we will hunt around to find the hill

with the pine-trees and the cottage. We will soon have the little prince safe and sound!"

And so, the very day after he had set free his kite, Rollo saw a large company of soldiers riding swiftly over the lonely country that lay around the hill. Griffin heard the hooves of the horses and came to see who was galloping near.

"You can't escape!" cried Rollo. "They are surrounding the cottage. And look, they've got dogs with them – so even if you make yourself invisible they will smell you and catch you!"

So Griffin was captured, and the little prince taken home in triumph. He went to his castle, and the magician went to prison.

"What did I tell you, Griffin?" called Rollo as they parted. "Didn't I say that wickedness is always punished in the end, always! I'm not sorry for you, because you are not sorry for your wickedness! Good-bye!"

Griffin never guessed how it was that the soldiers knew where he had hidden Rollo, and all the years he was in prison he puzzled over it. But if he could have peeped into Prince Rollo's playroom, he would soon have guessed. For there, put in a place of honour on the wall, was the kite with the message on it – and below it the tail of messages, too.

Ah, Griffin, Rollo was too clever for you, and so was Sukie, too! You should hear them laugh about you when they play together, as they do every day now.

"It's not clever to be wicked!" says Rollo, and he's right, isn't he?

The Mean Old Man

ONCE upon a time there was a mean old man who wouldn't pay his bills. He owed Dame Rustle a lot of money for his newspapers. He owed Mr. Pork for his meat. Mother Cluck sent him a bill for milk and eggs time after time, but it was never paid. Really, it was dreadful!

One day they all put their heads together and laid a little plan. They bought a come-back spell from Witch Heyho and took bits of it back to their shops.

And the next day, when Dame Rustle gave a newspaper to old Mr. Mean, she tucked a bit of the come-back spell into it. When Mr. Pork sold him a string of sausages, he tucked a come-back spell into them too, and when Mother Cluck let Mr. Mean have a basket of new-laid eggs she carefully put a come-back spell at the bottom.

Well, old Mr. Mean set off home, carrying the basket of eggs, the sausages in paper, and the morning newspaper. But before he had got very far a curious thing happened. The come-back spell began to work!

It worked on the newspaper first. The paper grew small legs and tried to get away from under Mr. Mean's arm! Mr. Mean could not think why it kept slipping. He kept pushing it back under his arm – but still that newspaper wriggled and wriggled and at last it fell to the ground. No sooner did it fall on to its feet than it tore off down the pavement as fast as it could go, running back to Dame Rustle's!

"Gracious!" said Mr. Mean in surprise. "How the wind is taking that paper along, to be sure."

Well, the next thing that happened was most annoying to Mr. Mean. The come-back spell began to work in the sausages, and they wriggled out of their wrapping, which fell to the ground. Mr. Mean stopped to pick it up – and, hey presto! that string of sausages leapt to the ground and tore off on tiny legs as fast as could be. All the dogs in the street barked to see them rushing along like a large brown caterpillar – but they knew better than to touch sausages with a come-back spell in them.

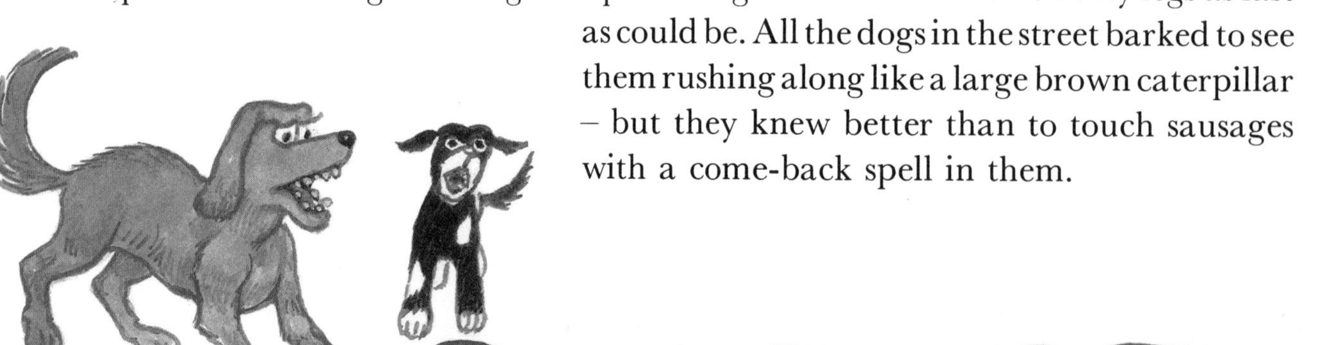

"Jumping pigs!" said Mr. Mean in the greatest alarm. "Now, what's the meaning of that? Look at those sausages! Do they think they are in for a race or what? Something funny is about this morning – or else I'm dreaming!"

He pinched himself hard to see if he was dreaming – but the pinch hurt so much that he knew he was wide awake. So on he went again, wondering what could be the matter with everything.

"Anyhow, the eggs are all right," he said, looking down at them. But even as he spoke the come-back spell began to work in them, too. One by one those eggs grew chicken-legs and climbed up to the rim of the basket, ready to jump out!

"Oh no, you don't!" said Mr. Mean, grabbing at the top egg. "No jumping about like that, eggs, or you'll break."

But the eggs took no notice of Mr. Mean. One by one they jumped out of the basket and tore back to Mother Cluck's as fast as they could. It was a most astonishing sight to see.

Mr. Mean was furious. "There's some spell at work," he cried. "Someone's playing a trick on me!"

"Perhaps, Mr. Mean," said Mrs. Twinkle-toes, who was just nearby, "perhaps you haven't paid for those things. They have gone back to be sold to someone who *will* pay for them."

Mr. Mean went home in a rage. He wasn't going to pay his bills till he wanted to. Nobody could make him take his money out of the bank if he didn't want to!

But, oh dear! What a life he led the next few days! His new hat jumped clean off his head and hurried back to the hatter's. His new shoes wriggled off his feet and ran back to the shoe shop with such a clatter that everyone turned to see what was making the noise – and of course they saw old Mr. Mean standing in his socks looking as wild as could be – and, dear me, he had such a big hole in one toe.

Even the bananas he bought hopped out of the bag they were in and galloped back to the greengrocer's. Soon the people of the town followed Mr. Mean when he did his shopping, so that they could see the strange sight of everything racing back to the shops afterwards.

Well, Mr. Mean knew there was nothing else to be done but to pay his bills. So he took some money out of the bank and paid them all, every one. Then his goods stopped behaving in such a strange manner and stayed in their bags and baskets till he got home.

And you may be sure they will behave all right just so long as he pays his bills – but as the shopkeepers still have some of the come-back spell left, they will play old Mr. Mean some more tricks if he begins to be mean again.

Witch Heyho still has plenty of come-back spells to sell, so if you know of anyone who needs one, just send a message to her!

"I Don't Want To!"

ONCE upon a time there was a little girl called Fanny. She was eight years old, and she had been spoilt. She had been ill quite a lot, and because her mother had been sorry for her, she had let Fanny have her own way far too much.

Whenever she asked Fanny to do something she didn't like, the little girl would say "I don't want to!" and would pout and frown.

"Will you go and post this letter for me?" her mother would say. And Fanny would make the usual answer:

"I don't want to!"

Well, if you say a thing like that often enough, you just can't stop, and soon Fanny was saying "I don't want to!" a hundred times a day.

"What a spoilt child!" people said. "Really she is most unpleasant!"

Her Granny spoke sternly to her. "Fanny," she said, "I don't like this habit you have of saying 'I don't want to!' to everything. Do try to stop."

"I don't want to," said Fanny at once.

Well, well – what can you do with a child like that!

Now one day Fanny went across the fields and took a wrong turning. Soon she found herself outside a strange little house. A well stood nearby and an old woman was turning the handle that drew up the bucket of water. She saw Fanny and beckoned to her.

"Little girl, come and help me to get this water!"

"I don't want to!" said Fanny at once.

The old woman frowned. She wound up the bucket, took it off the hook, and set it down.

"You could carry it for me into the house," she said. "I'm rather tired to-day."

"I don't want to!" said Fanny, of course.

"Well, what a horrid child!" said the old dame. "You can't seem to say anything else but 'I don't want to!' Can't you say something pleasant for a change?"

"I don't want to!" said Fanny.

"Very well – don't!" said the old woman. "Say 'I don't want to!' and nothing else! Maybe you will soon want to change!"

And with that she went up the path to her cottage, opened the door, went inside and shut the door after her. Fanny felt a bit frightened. She remembered that the old woman had green eyes. Perhaps she was one of the fairy folk!

She ran off, and soon found her path. She went back home – and on the way she met Jane, a school-friend.

"Fanny! Come and play with me after tea and see my new doll!" called Jane.

"I don't want to!" said Fanny, much to her own surprise, because she did want to, very much indeed. Jane had told everyone at school about her new doll which could stand up by itself, and say "Mamma!"

"All right, don't come then!" said Jane, offended. "I'll ask Mary."

Fanny walked home, upset. Her mother met her at the door.

"Fanny dear, go and get yourself some sweets before you come in," she said. "You didn't have your pocket money last week. Go and spend it now."

"I don't want to!" said Fanny, and made her mother stare in surprise. Fanny stared at her mother too. She hadn't meant to say that! She loved sweets and it was fun to go and buy them. She wanted to say "I *do* want to!" but all her tongue said was "I don't want to!" once again.

"My dear child, if you don't want to, you needn't!" said her mother. "How tiresome you are sometimes! I will give the money to John next door."

Fanny walked up to her bedroom, almost in tears. She passed the cook on the way.

"I'm making cakes," said Cook. "Come along down and scrape the dishes out, Miss Fanny."

Now this was a thing that Fanny simply loved doing. But, as you can guess, all her tongue would answer was "I don't want to!"

"Well, I thought it would be a treat for you," said the cook, offended, and she marched downstairs with her head in the air.

Poor Fanny! This was a dreadful day for her. It seemed as if everyone was offering something nice for her to do. And all she could say was "I don't want to!".

In the end everyone was cross with her, and her mother sent her to bed. "Go up to bed and stay there!" said Mummy.

"I don't want to!" said Fanny. But she had to go all the same.

Now when she was in bed, crying under the blankets, there came a tap at the door – and who should come in but the old woman who had been by the well.

"Good evening," she said to Fanny. "How have you been getting on with that tongue of yours? Wouldn't it be nice to speak properly again?"

Fanny couldn't answer, because she knew that if she did, her tongue would say "I don't want to!" And she did badly want to speak properly again – very, very badly.

"Well now," said the old dame. "I'll make a bargain with you. If you try to be a nice little girl, and will not be spoilt and rude, I'll make your tongue right again. But I warn you that if you say 'I don't want to' more than once in a day, the spell will come back again and you'll find you can't say anything else but that!"

"Thank you," said Fanny. "I'm sorry I was rude to you. I won't be rude or spoilt any more."

"That's the way to talk!" said the old dame, and she smiled. "Good-bye! Come and see me another day, and maybe your tongue will say something nicer to me than 'I don't want to!'."

Well, Fanny found it very hard to get out of her bad habit, but as she knew quite well that the spell would come back if she said "I don't want to" more than once in a day, she was very, very careful. The spell hasn't come back, so maybe she will be all right now.

She is trying to find the old woman's cottage again to tell her that she has cured herself. I wish I could go with her. I'd like to see the old dame's green eyes twinkling at me, wouldn't you?

Adventures of the Sailor Doll

ONCE there was a sailor doll, and he lived in Janet's nursery. She was very fond of him, and he went everywhere with her. He was such a smart doll, with a blue velvet uniform and a nice sailor collar and round hat. He had a pink, smiling face, and was the most cheerful person you can imagine!

And then one day a dreadful thing happened to him. A puppy came into the garden where Janet was playing, and began to romp about. Janet was frightened and fled indoors. She left her sailor doll behind her on the grass! Oh, dear, what a pity!

The puppy saw the doll smiling up at him, and he picked it up in his teeth. He threw the doll into the air. The sailor stopped smiling, for he was frightened.

The doll came down on the grass. The puppy picked him up again and began to nibble him. He nibbled his hat and made a hole. He nibbled his sailor collar and tore it. He nibbled a shoe and got it off.

And then he did a really *dreadful* thing. He chewed one of the sailor's arms off! He bit it right off, and there it lay on the grass beside the poor scared doll.

Then there came a whistling, and the puppy's master came along. The puppy heard the whistling, ran to the gate, and darted out to his master. Off he went down the road, galloping along, leaving behind him the poor chewed sailor.

Well, Janet's mother very soon came out to clear up her little girl's toys, and she saw the sailor doll lying on the grass with his arm beside him. She was very sorry. She picked him up and looked at him.

"I'm afraid you're no more use," she said. "You'll have to go into the dust-bin, sailor. You are all chewed, and you have lost an arm."

She put him on the seat and went on collecting the other toys. The sailor doll was so horrified at hearing he would have to go into the dust-bin that he lay and shivered. Then, seeing that Janet's mother was not looking, he quietly picked up his chewed arm, put it into his pocket, jumped down from the seat, and slipped away into the bushes. *He* wasn't going to be put into the dust-bin! Not he!

Janet's mother was surprised to find he had gone; but it was getting dark, so she went in with the other toys and didn't bother any more about the sailor. As soon as she had gone the sailor slipped out of the bushes and ran down the

garden path. He went into the field at the end of the garden and walked over the grass.

He didn't know where he was going. He was just running away from the dust-bin. He went on and on, and soon the moon came up and lighted everything clearly. Still he walked on. He met a hedgehog ambling along looking for beetles, and a mole with a long snout, and heard two mice quarrelling in the hedges. Still he went on – and at last he could go no further. He was really quite tired out. He had come to a little stream, and being a sailor doll he loved the sound of water.

"I think I'll settle down here for the night," thought the sailor. "I can go on in the morning. I think I am far enough away from that dust-bin now."

So he crept under a dock leaf and lay down. Soon the moon went behind a great cloud, and it began to rain. A goblin crept under the dock leaf to shelter and, finding the sailor there, pushed him away. So the rain poured down on the poor sailor doll and soaked him through. He was so tired didn't wake up till the morning – and then what a shock he had!

His sailor suit had shrunk in the rain and was now far too small for him. His hat had shrunk too, and looked very silly perched right on top of his head. His trouser legs were up to his knees, and his coat would no longer meet. He really looked dreadful.

He walked out into the sunshine, and how he sneezed, for he had caught a cold in the rain:

"A-tishoo! A-tishoo!"

"Hallo, hallo!" said a small voice, and the sailor doll saw an elf peeping at him. "What's the matter with *you*? You look a bit of a scarecrow! What are you?"

"I am supposed to be a sailor doll," said the sailor humbly. "I know I look dreadful now."

"Well, you've got a bad cold," said the elf. "Come into this rabbit-hole and I'll make a fire and dry you."

The doll followed the elf, and to his enormous surprise he saw that down the rabbit-hole was a small door, neatly fitted into the side of the burrow. The elf opened the door, and inside was a cosy room with a fire laid ready for lighting. Soon it was crackling away cheerfully. The doll dried his clothes and felt more cheerful, especially when the elf brought him some hot lemonade and some ginger biscuits. Aha! This was good!

"Now you must get on to my sofa and have a good rest," said the elf kindly. "You can stay here all day in the warmth, if you like."

So he did; and when the night came, the elf said he might sleep there too.

"I am going to a boating party," she said. "It's being held on the stream. So you can sleep here all night, if you like. I shan't be back till dawn."

"A boating party!" said the sailor doll, excited. "Oh, can't I come?"

"No, it would be better for you to stay here in the warm and get rid of your cold," said the elf.

She put on a cape and ran out. The doll wished he knew what a boating party was like. He had never been to one. He opened the door and went into the rabbit-hole to see if he could hear any happy shouts and screams from the boating party. At first he heard laughter and shouts – and then he heard a great crying:

"Oh! Oh! You horrid frogs! Go away! You are spoiling our party!"

Then there came a sound of splashing and screaming. Whatever could be happening?

The doll ran out into the moonlight – and he saw a strange sight. The elves had many little silver boats on the stream, and a great crowd of green frogs had popped up to sink the little boats.

One after another they were pulled under by the mischievous frogs. The elves flew out of the boats as soon as they began to sink, but they were most unhappy because they had lost their pretty boats, and the party was spoilt.

The sailor doll ran to the bank in anger. "How dare you do such a thing, frogs?" he cried. "I will go and tell the ducks to come here and eat you!"

The frogs swam off in fright. But not a single boat was left!

"A-tishoo!" said the sailor doll. "I *am* sorry I didn't come before!"

"Our party is spoilt!" wept the little elves. "We have no more boats – and oh, we were having *such* fun!"

A bright idea came into the sailor doll's head.

"I say," he said, "I know how to make boats out of paper. They float very well

too. I used to watch Janet making them. If you can get me some paper, I could tell you how to make them."

The elves gave a shout of delight and ran off. Soon they came back with all sorts of pieces of paper, and they placed them in front of the doll.

"I wish I could make the boats for you," he said, "but, you see, I have only one arm, so I can't. But I will tell you how to do it. Now – fold your paper in half to begin with."

The elves all did as he said, and soon there were dozens of little paper boats all ready to float on the river. Lovely!

The elves launched them, and presently another boating party was going on. The frogs didn't dare to appear this time, so everything went off merrily.

In the middle of the party a big ship with silver sails came floating down the stream.

"Look! Look! The Fairy King and Queen are sailing to-night, too!" shouted the elves in glee.

"Let us float round them in our paper boats and give them a hearty cheer!"

So they did; and the King and Queen were *most* astonished to see such a fleet of boats appearing round their ship, full of cheering elves.

"Go to the bank and anchor there," the King commanded. So the ship headed for the bank and very soon it anchored there, and the elves went on board to bow and curtsy to their majesties.

"Who has taught you how to make these lovely boats?" asked the Queen, in surprise. "I have never seen any like them before!"

"The sailor doll did," said the little elf who had helped the doll. She told the King all about the boating party spoilt by the frogs, and how the doll had taught them to make paper boats.

"Bring him here!" commanded the King. But the sailor doll was shy and didn't want to go before their majesties.

"I am all dirty and wet, and my suit is too small for me," he said. "Besides, I have lost an arm, and I am ashamed of having only one. Also, I have a bad cold, and I should not like to give it to the King or Queen. A-tishoo!"

So the elf told the King what the doll had said, and the King nodded his head.

"See that the doll is given a new suit," he said, "and do what you can about his arm, elf. Then send him to me at the palace. I want to speak to him about something very important."

The elf took the surprised sailor doll back to her cosy home in the burrow. She looked him up and down and pursed up her tiny mouth.

"You'll have to have a new suit altogether," she said. "It wouldn't be any good patching up the one you have on. I can get you a new hat made too. The only thing that worries me is your arm. I don't know how I can get you one to match your own."

"Oh, I've got my old one in my pocket," said the sailor doll, and he pulled out his chewed arm.

"Oh, splendid!" said the elf. "Now look here, sailor, just take off all your old clothes, whilst I go to fetch little Stitchaway the Pixie to measure you for a new suit. You can put on my dressing-gown. Sit by the fire and drink some more hot lemon. Your cold seems better already."

She went out. The doll took off his old, dirty suit, put on the elf's little dressing-gown, and sat down by the fire. He was very happy. Things seemed to be turning out all right, after all.

Soon the elf came back with a small pixie who was covered with pin-cushions, scissors and needle-books. With her she carried a great bunch of bluebells.

"Good-day, sailor," she said. "I shall have to make your suit of bluebells. I hope you won't mind, but that is the only blue I have at the moment. Now, stand up, and let me measure you."

It didn't take long to measure the sailor. No sooner was this done than two more pixies appeared. One was a shoe-maker, and he soon fitted the sailor with a pair of fine black boots. Then the other pixie, who was a hatter, and wore about twenty different hats piled on his head, tried them all on the sailor, and found a little round one that fitted him exactly. It had a blue feather in it, but the elf said that it looked very nice, so the sailor left it in.

"Now where's your arm?" said the elf. The doll took his arm from the shelf where he had put it whilst he was being measured. The elf fitted it neatly into his shoulder, said a few magic words, and let go. The arm was as good as ever! The doll could use it just as well as he could use the other one. He was so delighted!

In two days' time the dressmaker elf came back with the grandest blue sailor suit of bluebells that you can imagine! When the sailor dressed himself in it, he did feel smart. The elf looked at him in admiration.

"You look like the captain of a ship," she said. "Now come along to the palace, and we'll see what the King wants."

Well, what *do* you suppose His Majesty wanted? The captain of his fairy fleet was old, and was going to leave the sea and live in a little cottage with his wife. The King wanted another captain – and that was why he had sent for the sailor doll.

"Will you be my new captain?" he asked him. "You look so cheerful, always smiling – and the way you sent off those wicked frogs, and taught the elves how to make new boats, was wonderful. I'd very much like you to be my new captain."

"Oh, Your Majesty, it's too good to be true!" cried the doll, blushing all over his smiling face. "I promise you I will do my very best."

"Very well. You are my captain, then!" said the King. "Now come and have tea with the Queen and our children. They are all longing to know how to make paper boats."

And now the sailor doll is very important indeed, and everyone in Fairyland salutes him when he goes by. You should see him commanding his ship too! You would never think he was once a poor chewed doll who was nearly put in a dustbin!

The Unkind Children

Ping! A stone came flying through the air and almost hit a little sparrow sitting on the fence. It flew away with a chirrup of fright.

"Nearly got that bird," said Robert. "Your turn now, Winnie."

Ping! Winnie's stone hit the wall, and the next-door cat, who was lying asleep there, leapt off with a loud yell.

"Those unkind children again!" she said.

Soon every bird and animal nearby was warned that Winnie and Robert were throwing stones again. Not a single one would go near them. They all hated the two unkind children who loved to throw stones at any living thing.

"Nothing to throw stones at!" said Winnie. "Let's go for a walk. Maybe we shall find some birds down the lane."

Off they went, their hands full of small stones. They kept a sharp look-out for any bird in the hedge or on the telegraph wires.

They came to a low wall that ran round a garden. Winnie stopped and pulled Robert's arm.

"Look – what a funny bird! Do you see it?" Robert looked. He saw a very strange-looking bird indeed. It was on top of the wall. It was red, with yellow wings and a bright green tail.

"See if you can hit it!" said Winnie. Robert took a stone, and aimed it carefully. It struck the bird full on the back!

"Good shot!" said Winnie.

And then a dreadful thing happened! Somebody stood up from behind the wall – somebody wearing a hat which was trimmed with the red and yellow bird! The bird hung sideways from the hat now, looking very strange.

"Oooh! It was a bird in a hat!" said Winnie, frightened.

A big woman glared at the two children. She wore a red cloak, the bird-trimmed hat, and big spectacles on her nose.

"Come here!" she rapped out. "It's time you were taught a lesson! I'm Mrs. Do-the-Same-to-You! Maybe you've heard of me?"

The children hadn't, but they didn't like the sound of her at all. They turned to run away. But in a trice Mrs. Do-the-Same-to-You was over the wall and was holding them firmly by their arms. She had a big bag with her. She opened it and popped the two unkind children into it. It wasn't a bit of good struggling. They couldn't get out.

Mrs. Do-the-Same-to-You took them to her cottage in the middle of the wood. She shook the children out of her bag on to the grass. Bump! They fell out and yelled.

She took a whistle from her pocket and blew on it. At once a small army of brownies, not much bigger than dolls, came running from the wood.

"These are the Brownie King's pea-shooters," she said to the children. "They don't get enough practice at shooting peas at people. You don't seem to mind hitting others with stones, so I don't expect you'll mind if you are shot at with peas! It will be excellent practice for the pea-shooters."

The children didn't like the sound of this at all. They could see no way of escape, because there was a high wall round the garden, and Mrs. Do-the-Same-to-You stood by the only gate. They tried to run behind a bush.

The brownie pea-shooters all had little blow-pipes and bags of hard, dried peas. Quick as lightning, they slipped peas into their mouths and blew them hard out of the blow-pipes or pea-shooters.

Ping! The first one hit Winnie on the nose.

Ping! Another one hit Robert on the ear.

Ping! Ping! Ping! Three peas hit the children hard on hand, knee and neck. They yelled.

"This is good sport!" cried the little brownies. "Are you sure it's all right for us to practise on these children, Mrs. Do-the-Same-to-You?"

"Oh, quite," she said. "I found them throwing stones at birds. They can't object to you shooting peas at them! After all, you are doing much the same thing, but using peas instead of stones."

"Stop! Stop!" cried the children. "The peas hurt. They sting! Oh, stop!"

"Well, don't stones hurt too?" asked Mrs. Do-the-Same-to-You. "Perhaps you would rather the pea-shooters shot stones?"

"Oh no, oh no!" cried Winnie. "Stones would be worse. Oh, let us go! That pea nearly went into my eye."

Ping! Ping! Ping! Ping! The little pea-shooters were having a fine time. The children dodged here and there, they tried to hide behind trees and bushes, they ran to corners, but always the brownies followed them, blowing hard peas at them and hardly ever missing. Soon the children were covered with red spots where the peas had hit them, and they began to feel very sorry for themselves indeed.

Mrs. Do-the-Same-to-You went indoors to put her kettle on to boil. As soon as Robert saw that she had left the gate, he took Winnie's hand and dragged her there. In a trice he had it open and the two children shot through it.

After them poured the delighted brownies, shooting peas as hard as they could! They chased Winnie and Robert all the way to edge of the wood. Ping, ping, ping, ping, went the peas. You should have heard the children yell!

They got home at last, tears running down their faces. They rubbed the red places that the peas had hit.

"Horrid little brownies!" sobbed Winnie.

"Unkind little creatures!" wept Robert.

"How dare they, how dare they?" cried Winnie. "Just look at all the red marks on my face, hands and knees! I'm hurting all over!"

"Wait till I see that nasty Mrs. Do-the-Same-to-You!" yelled Robert. "I'll tell her what I think of her! I'll throw a big stone at her!"

But when he met her, he didn't say a word and he didn't throw a stone. In fact, neither he nor Winnie have ever thrown a stone at anything again. They know now how it hurts to have something hitting you hard. They still have little red spots where those peas struck them.

I don't feel a bit sorry for them, do you?

Gooseberry Whiskers

THERE was once a rascally gnome who sold fine paint-brushes to the fairies. No brushes were half as good as his, for the hairs in them were so fine and strong.

"Where do you get them from?" asked the elves one day. But the gnome wouldn't tell them.

"It's a secret," he said. "Perhaps I make them out of moonbeams drawn out long and thin, and snipped off in short pieces!"

"You don't!" cried the elves. "Oh *do* tell us your secret!"

But he never would – and the reason was that he was afraid to. He got the hairs from sleeping caterpillars, and such a thing was not allowed in Fairyland, as you may guess. Many caterpillars were covered with soft fine hairs, and by pulling a few from this one and a few from that, the little gnome soon had enough for a new brush.

One spring-cleaning time there was a great demand for his brushes. All through May the elves came to buy from him and the gnome could hardly find enough caterpillars to pull hairs from!

He began to pull more than a few hairs from each. Once he took quite a handful, and the caterpillar woke up with a squeak.

Another furry caterpillar woke up one morning to find that he was quite bald. He hadn't a single hair left and he shivered with cold.

When the Queen passed by she stopped in surprise.

"But who could have taken your hairs away?" she asked the caterpillar. "No one would do such a naughty thing."

"Please, Your Majesty, someone must have done it last night," said the caterpillar.

"And half *my* coat is gone too!" said another.

"And about thirty of my finest hairs have disappeared as well!" cried a third.

"This must be looked into," said the Queen, sternly.

She called to her guards and spoke to them. "Twelve of you must remain here to look after these caterpillars," she commanded. "You can hide under the hedge, and watch for the thief. Catch him and punish him well."

The caterpillars crawled to their leaves. Now at last they would be safe! The twelve guards looked about for good hiding-places, and then played a game of snap until night-time, for they felt sure there would be no sign of the thief until darkness fell. The caterpillars were so interested in the game that they called "Snap!" when they shouldn't, and made the guards quite cross.

"Don't interfere," said the captain. "*We* are playing, not you. You eat your juicy leaves, and don't disturb us or we will leave you to the robber!"

When night came the soldiers squeezed themselves into their hiding-places and kept watch. The night was dark, and it was difficult for them to see an inch in front of their noses. Just the night for a robber to come!

Time went on. No thief. Ten o'clock came, eleven o'clock. Still no thief. The guards began to yawn. Surely the robber would not come now.

But at that very moment the little gnome was out on his rounds, looking for furry caterpillars. He was hunting under the leaves, down the stalks, on the ground, and everywhere. He didn't know that anyone was lying in wait for him.

He was very silent. His feet made no sound as he crept along, and he didn't even rustle a leaf.

"Where are all the caterpillars to-night?" he thought. "I can't seem to find any!"

From bush to bush he went, feeling along the leaves, and at last he really did find a large furry caterpillar, peacefully sleeping.

"Good!" thought the gnome. "This one has a fine crop of hairs! I can make a fine brush from them."

He grabbed a big handful from the back of the sleeping caterpillar, and pulled hard. The caterpillar woke up with a loud squeak. "Eee, eee, eee!" it cried.

At once all the guards sprang up and shouted loudly. "The robber, the robber!"

The gnome fled away in terror, holding all the hairs in his hand. The guards ran after him, and went crashing through the woods into the palace gardens. Up and down the paths they went, searching for the thief. Where was he? Where had he gone?

The little gnome had found a prickly hiding-place under a big gooseberry bush. He crouched there in fright, wondering what would happen to him if he was found. In his hand he still held the caterpillar hairs. Whatever could he do with them?

"The guards mustn't find them in my hand," he thought. "And I daren't throw them away, for they are sure to be found. What *can* I do?"

He put out his hand and felt about. He touched two or three big fat gooseberries – and then an idea came to him. He would stick the hairs on them, for surely no one would think of looking on the fruit for caterpillar hairs!

In a trice he was sticking the hairs on the green smooth surface of the gooseberries. He made them all hairy and whiskery, and just as he had finished, somebody came down the path near-by, and flashed a lantern on to him.

"Here's someone!" they cried. "Here's the thief! Quick, come and get him!"

The gnome was dragged out and searched. No hairs were found on him, but in his pocket were two brushes that he had forgotten about – and they were made of caterpillar hairs!

"Spank him, spank him well!" cried the captain. "That will teach him not to steal! Then turn him out of Fairyland for ever!"

So the gnome was spanked very hard, and taken to the gates of Fairyland. They were shut behind him, and out he went, weeping bitterly.

No one has heard of him since – but from that day to this gooseberries have always grown whiskers. If you don't believe me, go and look for yourself!

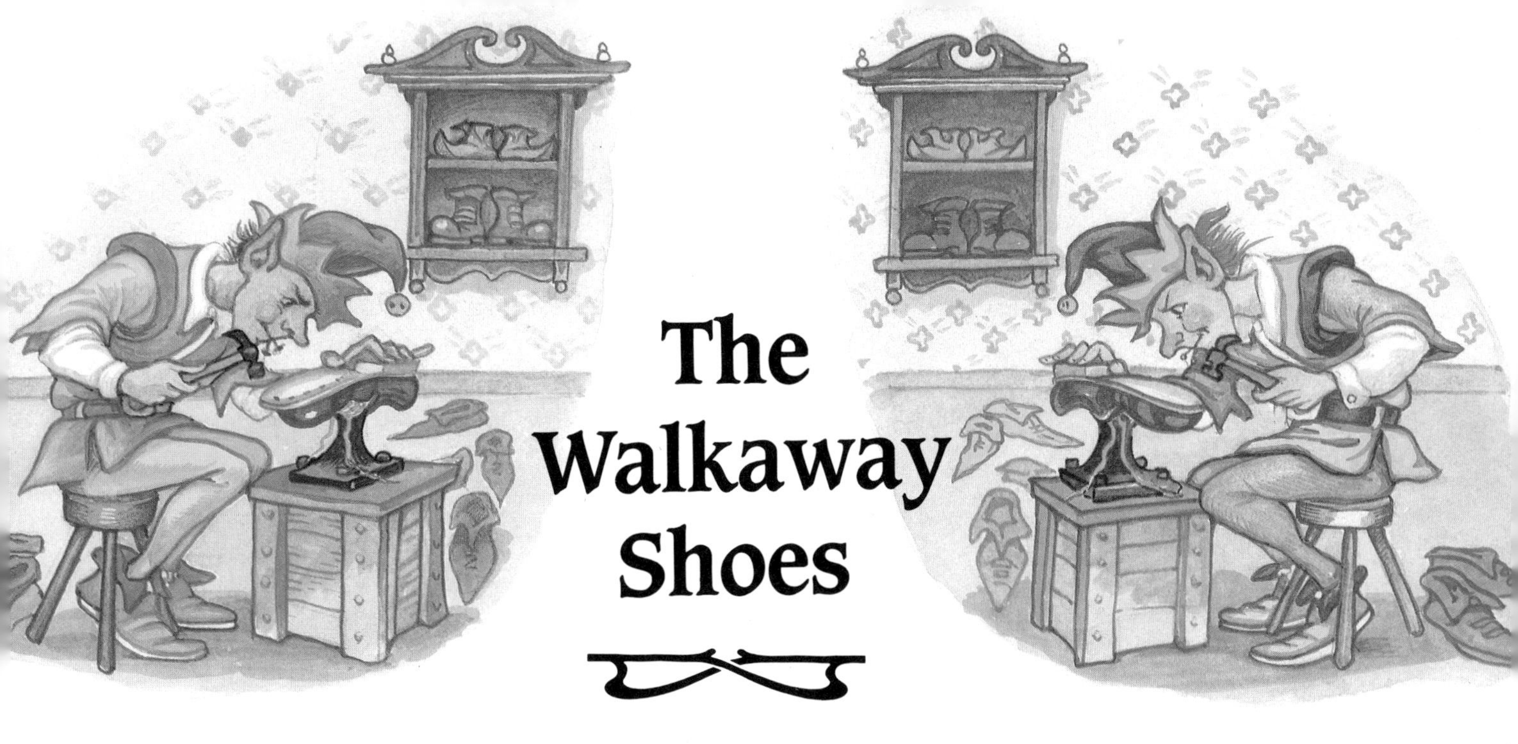

The Walkaway Shoes

"You know, the two new brownies who have set up a shop in Toadstool Cottage make the most beautiful shoes," said Pixie Light-Feet to Limpy the gnome. "You should get them to make you a pair of shoes for your poor old feet, Limpy. Then you could walk well again."

Limpy went to see the two brownies, Slick and Sharpy. They bowed and smiled and welcomed him.

"Yes, yes, Limpy. We will make you such a comfortable pair of shoes that you won't want to take them off even when you go to bed!" they said.

Well, they made him a red pair with green laces, and they were so beautiful and so comfortable that Limpy went around telling everyone about them.

Soon all the little folk of the village were going to Slick and Sharpy for their shoes, and the two brownies worked hard the whole day long. They were pleased.

"Our money-box is getting full," said Slick. "Is it time we did our little trick, Sharpy?"

"It is," said Sharpy. "Now, in future we put a walkaway spell into every pair of shoes. Don't forget!"

Dame Shuffle came that day and ordered a pair of blue boots. "We've got just what you want!" said Slick, showing her a pair. "Try them on!"

She tried them on, and they fitted her so well that she bought them at once, grumbling at the price. "I'll wrap them up for you," said Sharpy, and he took them into the other room to find some paper. He slipped a little yellow powder into each boot and then wrapped them up and took them to Dame Shuffle. Off she went, and wore them out to tea that afternoon.

"Beautiful!" said Mother Nid-Nod. "I'll get a pair from Slick and Sharpy, too."

"So will I," said Mr. Tiptap. And the next day off they went to buy a pair each. But on the way they met Dame Shuffle, who looked very worried.

"Someone came in the night and stole my boots," she said. "My beautiful new boots that cost so much. They are quite, quite gone."

"Oh dear – robbers must be about," said Mr. Tiptap. "I shall be very careful of mine when I get them."

He got a pair of red shoes and Mother Nid-Nod got a pair of brown shoes with green buckles. Slick and Sharpy grinned at one another when both customers had gone.

"Did you put the walkaway spell in them?" said Slick.

Sharpy nodded. "Yes, both pairs will be back again to-night!" he said. "And we'll put them into our sack ready to take away with us when our money-box is quite full."

That night the spell inside Mother Nid-Nod's brown shoes and Mr. Tiptap's red ones began to work. Mother Nid-Nod heard a little shuffling sound and thought it was mice. She called her cat into her bedroom at once.

"Cinders," she said, "catch the mice in this room while I am asleep." So Cinders watched – but instead of mice running about he saw Mother Nid-Nod's shoes walk to the door, and all the way downstairs, and hop out of the open kitchen window. How scared he was!

Mr. Tiptap's shoes did exactly the same thing. The old man didn't hear anything, he was so sound asleep. But the brown owl in the woods suddenly saw a pair of red shoes walking along all by themselves, and was so surprised that he almost fell off the branch he was sitting on.

"Who-who-who is that?" he hooted. "Is there someone invisible walking in those shoes? Who-who-who is it?"

But it wasn't anyone, of course. It was just the walkaway spell in the shoes sending them back to the two bad brownies.

The people of the village began to get very upset. Everyone who bought lovely new shoes from Slick and Sharpy lost them in the night. And then, when they brought their old shoes to be mended and took them home again, those went, too!

Slick and Sharpy just slipped walkaway spells in the mended shoes as well – and, of course, they walked away to the little toadstool house the very next night!

"Our money-box is full," said Slick. "Most of the shoes we have made for the people here have come back to us – as well as a lot of their old shoes that we mended."

"Good," said Sharpy. "Let's go to another village now. We can settle in and do no work for a long time because we shall have so many pairs of boots and shoes to sell!"

"We'll just make this last pair of high boots for Mr. Bigfeet," said Slick. "He has promised us five gold pieces for them – so that means we will have a lot of money from him – and if we put the usual walkaway spell in the boots we shall have those, too, because they will come back to us to-night!"

Mr. Bigfeet called for the boots that afternoon and paid for them. "I hope no one comes to steal *these* boots!" he said. "They're beautiful!"

Now, Bigfeet had a little servant called Scurry-About. She was a timid little goblin, very fond of her big master. She thought the boots were lovely, and she polished them till they shone that night.

"Oh, Master!" she said. "I hope no one will steal them!"

"Well, see that they don't!" said Bigfeet and went up to bed. Scurry-About always slept down in the kitchen. The boots were there, too. She looked at them.

"Oh dear – I sleep so very soundly that if anyone comes to steal them I would never hear!" she said. "I know what I'll do! I'll go to sleep wearing them! Then if a robber comes he will have to pull them off my feet and I shall wake up and scream!"

Well, she curled herself up in her small bed with the big boots on her feet. They reached right up to her knees! She fell sound asleep.

And in the night the walkaway spell began to work! The boots wanted to walk back to Slick and Sharpy. But they couldn't, because Scurry-About was wearing them. They began to wriggle and struggle to get themselves off her feet.

She woke up at once. "Who's pulling off the boots? Master, Master, come quickly, someone is stealing your boots!" she cried.

Bigfeet woke up at once and came scrambling down to the kitchen. He was most surprised to find Scurry-About wearing his boots. And dear me, what was this? They leapt off her bed, taking her with them – and then began to walk to the window. Up to the sill they jumped, and then tried to leap out.

But Scurry-About was still in them, and she screamed because she was stuck halfway through the window. "Help, help! The boots are taking me away!"

And then Bigfeet suddenly knew what was happening! "There's a spell in them!" he cried. "A walkaway spell, put there by those tiresome brownies – the rogues! Scurry-About, I'm going to open the window wide and let the boots take you away with them – but I'll follow close behind!"

"Oh, Master! Help me!" squealed poor little Scurry-About, and woke up all the villagers around, so that they threw on their dressing-gowns and came hurrying to see what was happening.

Bigfeet opened his window wide. The boots set off at top speed with Scurry-About's feet in them, taking her along, too. Through the wood and into the lane and down the street – and right up to Toadstool Cottage went those big top-boots!

And there they kicked at the door to be let in. Scurry-About was crying, and Bigfeet was shouting in rage. All the other villagers were calling out in amazement.

"See! They are walking off to Slick and Sharpy! The wicked brownies! Wait till we get hold of them!"

Slick and Sharpy heard all this and they were very frightened. Slick peeped out of the window. When he saw such an angry crowd he was alarmed.

"Quick, Sharpy," he said. "We must get out of the back door as soon as we can. Don't wait for anything – not even the money-box!"

So they fled down the stairs and opened the back door quietly. Out they went into the night and nobody saw them go.

The big boots kicked the door down and everyone went inside the house. Scurry-About pulled off the boots, crying.

"They've gone," said Bigfeet, looking all round.

"But they've left behind their money-box full of money – and sacks full of the boots they made for us!" said Mr. Tiptap, emptying them out. "Aha! It's *our* money because we paid it out to them – and they're *our* boots because they were made for us. How well-off we are!"

Nobody knew where Slick and Sharpy went to, and nobody cared. The villagers kept the boots and shoes and gave little Scurry-About two beautiful pairs for herself.

As for the money, it is being spent on a birthday present for the little Prince of Dreamland, who is five years old next week – he is going to have a box of wooden soldiers, who march away in rows – and then walk back again! You see, Bigfeet found the walkaway spell in a box at Toadstool Cottage – won't the little Prince be surprised!

What a Thing to Happen!

"GRANNY is going to have a little nap," Mummy said to Peter. "So don't make too much noise playing round her in the garden, will you!"

"No, I'll be very quiet," said Peter. "I'll read my new book." So he sat down with his book. Granny smiled at him from her deck-chair and then shut her eyes.

Peter read to the end of his book, and then he looked at Granny. If only she was awake he could ride his new little bicycle round the garden. What a pity it hadn't a bell! He did so want a nice, jingly bell, but Mummy had said he must save up for it.

He went over to look at his bicycle. It was still so new that he hadn't got used to it yet.

And then suddenly something most peculiar happened! A little man ran into the garden, wearing a long, pointed hat and pointed shoes. He had pointed ears too, and bright green eyes, and looked very like someone out of a fairy-tale book!

He saw Peter by his bicycle, looking at him in astonishment. He ran to him and called out loudly, "Will you lend me your bicycle, please?"

"Sh! My Granny's asleep," said Peter. "Why do you want my bicycle? It's almost a new one."

"Well, I want to go after someone who's stolen my black cat," said the little man. "It's a magic cat that helps me with my spells. And Sly-One came by this morning, saw my cat on the windowsill and ran off with him. I really must get him back."

Peter couldn't help feeling very astonished. "I can't let you borrow my bicycle," he said, "unless of course I go with you. You can ride it and I'll stand on the step behind."

"Right," said the little man, and leapt on the bicycle. Peter just had time to stand on the step and put his hands on the little man's shoulders – then away they went at top speed down the garden path!

"Look out for the hedge!" gasped Peter, but the little man took no notice at all – and to Peter's amazement the bicycle jumped right over the hedge as easily as anything! Really, this was all very very surprising!

"There he is, see – the fellow who stole my cat!" cried the little man suddenly, and far away in front Peter saw someone else, hurrying along, carrying

something black under his arm. On they went and on, and came to a little market-place which Peter had never seen before in any of his walks.

All kinds of strange folk were there, and the little man nearly knocked some of them down. "Where's your bicycle bell?" he shouted to Peter. "I can't find it. I simply must ring it to make people get out of my way or I shall lose my cat!"

"There isn't a bell," said Peter. "I'm so sorry. I'm saving up for one, you see!"

"A bicycle without a bell!" said the little man, quite crossly. "Never heard of such a thing! Get out of the way, you! Hey, there, make way, will you!"

At last they were out of the market-place and riding through a wood – and here the little rabbits kept popping across the path and the little man grew angrier than ever.

"How can I make them get out of the way without a bell!" he cried. "Wait – I must make one by magic." And he leapt off the bicycle, drew a circle in the dust with a twig, muttered some very magic words – and there, in the middle of the circle, appeared a bright, shining new bicycle bell. It really was most remarkable.

The little man fastened it to the bicycle handle, and away they went again, this time the bell ringing all the time – jingle-jingle-jingle, r-r-r-ring, r-r-r-ing!

"Ah – there's Sly-One! We've got him now!" said the little man, and to Peter's horror he rode straight into the back of the running man and knocked him flat!

He dropped the big black cat he was carrying and the cat at once jumped on to the little man's shoulder and began purring loudly.

"Get up!" said the little man to the thief, who was lying on the ground. "Get up! I'm taking you to the nearest policeman. How DARE you steal a magic cat!"

"Do you want my bicycle any more?" asked Peter. "It really won't take three of us."

"No, thank you. No, I don't," said the little man. "You ride home now. Many thanks for helping me to rescue my dear old cat."

"But I don't know my way home," said Peter, in alarm.

"Never mind! The bicycle does," said the little man. "Get on, and I'll give you a push, and it won't stop till you ride in at your garden gate. Go on now – I promise you it will take you home!"

Peter mounted the saddle and the little man gave him a push, and off went the bicycle at top speed. It certainly did seem to know the way! It went through the wood and came to the market. It went through that and into the fields, and Peter wondered how it could possibly know the way when *he* didn't!

He rang the bell loudly whenever he came across any rabbits, because he didn't want to hurt one, and it was plain that the bicycle didn't mean to stop until it was safely home. It even seemed to work the pedals itself, and they flew up and down, with Peter's feet doing their best to keep up with them.

He rode into his own garden, the bicycle having done a most surprising leap over the hedge again. Really, Peter was quite glad to be able to get off and lean it against a tree! He looked at Granny – and she was awake!

"Wherever have you been on your bicycle, dear?" she said, and Peter told her. How Granny laughed.

Pinkity and Old Mother Ribbony Rose

ONCE upon a time there lived an old witch called Mother Ribbony Rose. She kept a shop just on the borders of Fairyland, and because she sold such lovely things, the fairies allowed her to live there in peace.

She was very, very old, and very, very clever, but she wasn't very good. She was never kind to her neighbour, the Bee-Woman, and never helped the Balloon-Man, who lived across the road, and who was often very poor indeed when no one came to buy his lovely balloons.

But her shop was simply lovely. She sold ribbons, but they weren't just ordinary ribbons. There were blue ribbons, made of the mist that hangs over faraway hills, and sea-green ribbons embroidered with the diamond sparkles that glitter on sunny water. There were big broad ribbons of shiny silk, and tiny delicate ribbons of frosted spider's thread, and wonderful ribbons that tied their own bows.

The fairies and elves loved Mother Ribbony Rose's shop, and often used to come and buy there, whenever a fairy dance was going to be held and they wanted pretty things to wear.

One day Mother Ribbony Rose was very busy indeed.

"Good morning, Fairy Jasmin," she said, as a tall fairy, dressed in yellow, came into her shop. "What can I get you to-day?"

"Good morning, Mother Ribbony Rose," answered Jasmin politely. She didn't like the old witch a bit, but that didn't make any difference, she was always polite to her. "I would like to see the newest yellow ribbon you have, please, to match the dress I've got on to-day."

Mother Ribbony Rose pulled out a drawer full of yellow ribbons. Daffodil-yellows, orange-yellows, primrose-yellows, and all shining like gold.

"Here's a beauty!" she said, taking up a broad ribbon. "Would you like that?"

"No, thank you," answered Jasmin, "I want something narrower."

The witch pulled out another drawer and scattered the ribbons on the counter.

"Ah, here's one I like ever so!" exclaimed Jasmin, lifting up a long thin piece

of yellow ribbon, just the colour of her dress. "How much is it?"

"Two pieces of gold," answered Mother Ribbony Rose.

"Oh dear, you're terribly expensive," sighed Jasmin as she paid the money and took the ribbon.

Mother Ribbony Rose looked at all the dozens of ribbons scattered over the counter.

"Pinkity, Pinkity, Pinkity," she called in a sharp voice.

Out of the back of the shop came a tiny gnome.

"Roll up all these ribbons quickly, before anyone else comes in," ordered Mother Ribbony Rose, going into the garden.

Pinkity began rolling them up one by one. He did it beautifully, and so quickly that it was a marvel to watch him.

When all the ribbons were done, he went to the window and looked out. He saw fairies, gnomes, and pixies playing in the fields and meadows.

"Oh dear, dear, dear!" suddenly said Pinkity in a woebegone voice. "How I would love to go and play with the fairies. I'm so *tired* of rolling up ribbons." A large tear rolled down his cheek, and dropped with a splash on the floor.

"What's the matter, Pinkity?" suddenly asked a little voice.

Pinkity jumped and looked round. He saw a tiny fairy who had come into the shop and was waiting to be served.

"I'm so tired of doing nothing but roll up ribbons all day," explained Pinkity.

"Well, why don't you do something else?" asked the fairy.

"That's the worst of it. I've never done anything else all my life but roll up ribbons in Mother Ribbony's shop, and I *can't* do anything else. I can't paint, I can't dance, and I can't sing! All the other fairies would laugh at me if I went to play with them, for I wouldn't even know *how* to play!" sobbed Pinkity.

"Oh yes, you would! Come and try," said the little fairy, feeling very sorry for the lonely little gnome.

"Come and try! Come and try *what?*" suddenly said Mother Ribbony's voice, as she came in at the door.

"I was just asking Pinkity if he would come and play with us," answered the little fairy, feeling rather afraid of the witch's cross looks.

Mother Ribbony Rose snorted.

"Pinkity belongs to *me*," she said, "and he's much too busy in the shop, rolling up my beautiful ribbons all day, to have time to go and play with *you*. Besides, no one is allowed in Fairyland unless they can do some sort of work, and Pinkity can do nothing but roll up ribbons! I'm the only person who would keep him for that, for no one in Fairyland keeps a ribbon shop"; and the old witch pulled one of Pinkity's big ears.

"I should run away," whispered the little fairy to Pinkity when her back was turned.

"I wish I could! But I've nowhere to run to!" whispered back Pinkity in despair.

At that moment there came the sound of carriage wheels down the cobbled street, and old Mother Ribbony Rose poked her head out to see who it was.

"Mercy on us! It's the Lord High Chancellor of Fairyland, and he's coming here! Make haste, Pinkity, and get a chair for him!" cried the old witch, in a great flurry.

Sure enough it was.

The Chancellor strode into the shop, very tall and handsome, and sat down in the chair.

"Good morning," he said. "The King and Queen are holding a dance to-night, and they are going to make the wood pretty with ribbons and hang fairy lamps on them. The Queen has asked me to come and choose the ribbons for her. Will you show me some, please?"

"Certainly, certainly, your Highness!" answered Mother Ribbony Rose, pulling out drawer after drawer of colourful ribbons. Pinkity sighed as he watched her unroll ribbon after ribbon, and show it to the Chancellor.

"Oh dear! I'm sure it will take me hours and *hours* to roll up all that ribbon!" he thought to himself sadly.

"This is wonderful ribbon!" said the Chancellor admiringly. "I'll have fifty yards of this and fifty yards of that. Oh, and I'll have a hundred yards of this

glorious silver ribbon! It's just like moonlight. And send a hundred yards of this pink ribbon, please, too, and I'll have a ribbon archway with mauve lamps made, leading from the Palace to the wood. The Queen will be delighted!"

"Certainly!" answered the witch, feeling excited to think of all the gold she would get for such a lot of ribbon. "The pink ribbon is very expensive, your Highness. It's made of pink sunset clouds, mixed with almond blossom. I've only just got a hundred yards left!"

"That will just do," said the Chancellor, getting up to go. "Send it all to the Palace, please. And don't forget the *pink* ribbon, it's most important, *most* important!"

And off the Chancellor went to his carriage again.

Mother Ribbony Rose, who cared for gold more than she cared for anything else in the world, rubbed her hands together with delight.

"Now then, Pinkity!" she called. "Come here and roll up all this ribbon I've been showing to the Chancellor, and measure out all that he wants!"

Pinkity began rolling up the ribbon. He did it as quickly as ever he could, but even then it took him a long time. He measured out all the many yards that the Chancellor wanted, and folded them neatly. Then he got some paper and began to make out the bill.

"Hullo," said Pinkity, "the inkpot's empty. I must get the ink bottle down and fill it!"

He climbed up to the shelf where the big bottle of black ink was kept, and took hold of it.

But alas! Poor Pinkity slipped, and down fell the big bottle of ink on to the counter, where all the Chancellor's ribbon was neatly folded in piles! The cork came out, and before Pinkity knew what was happening all the ink upset itself on to the lovely ribbon, and stained it black in great patches.

In came old Mother Ribbony Rose.

"Pinkity! Pinkity! Look what you've done! And I haven't any more of that pink ribbon! You did it on purpose, I know you did, you naughty, naughty little gnome!" stormed the witch, stamping up and down.

Pinkity was dreadfully frightened. He was so frightened that, without thinking what he was doing, he jumped clean through the window and ran away!

He ran and ran and ran.

Then he lay down beneath a hedge and rested. Then he ran and ran and ran again, until it was night.

At last he came to a beautiful garden, lit by the moon, and quite empty, save for lovely flowers. It was the Queen's garden, but Pinkity did not know it.

"I'm free! I'm free!" cried Pinkity, throwing his hat in the air. "There's a dear little hole beneath this rock, and I'll hide there, and I'll NEVER go back to Mother Ribbony Rose."

He crept beneath the rock, shut his eyes and fell fast asleep.

Next morning he heard fairies in the garden and they were all talking excitedly.

"Yes, it was a naughty little gnome called Pinkity, who spoilt all the Queen's lovely ribbon," said one fairy.

"Yes, and he did it on purpose, old Mother Ribbony Rose says. Just fancy that!" said another.

"And the Chancellor says if anyone catches him, they're to take him to the Palace to be punished, and given back to Mother Ribbony Rose," said a third.

Pinkity lay and listened, and felt the tears rolling down his cheeks. He had so hoped that perhaps the fairies would help him.

All that day Pinkity hid, and at night he crept out into the lovely garden, and the flowers gave him honey to eat, for they were sorry for him.

For a long time Pinkity hid every day and only came out at night. One day he heard a group of fairy gardeners near by, talking hard.

"What *are* we to do about those little ferns?" they said. "As soon as they come up, their tiny fronds are spread out, and the frost *always* comes and bites them, and then they look horrid. It's just the same with the bracken over there!"

"It's so difficult to fold the fronds up tightly," said the fern fairies. "They *will* keep coming undone!"

"Well, we *must* think of something," said the gardeners decidedly. "The Queen simply loves her fernery, and she will be so upset if the frost bites the ferns again this year. Let's go and ask the rose gardeners if they can give us any hints."

That night Pinkity went over to the baby ferns and bracken and looked at them carefully. It was a very frosty night, and they looked very cold.

"*I* know! *I* know!" cried Pinkity, clapping his hands. "I'll *roll* them up like ribbons, and then they'll be quite warm and safe, and won't come undone till the frost is gone!"

So Pinkity started rolling each fern frond up carefully. It wasn't as easy as rolling ribbon, for the fronds had lots of the little bits to tuck in, but he worked hard and managed it beautifully. The baby ferns were very grateful, and so was the bracken.

"Thank you, thank you," they murmured. "We love being rolled up, and we're much warmer now."

Pinkity worked all night, and just as daylight came, he finished the very last piece of bracken and ran back to his hole to hide.

At six o'clock along came the gardeners. They stared and stared and stared at the ferns.

"Whatever has happened to them!" they cried in amazement. "They're rolled up just like ribbon!"

"What a splendid idea!" said the Head Gardener. "But who did it? Someone very kind and very clever must have done it!"

"*Who* did it? *Who* did it?" cried everyone.

Pinkety, trembling with excitement, crept out of his hiding-place.

"If you please," he said, "*I* did it!"

"Why, Pinkity! It's Pinkity, the naughty little gnome!" cried the fairies.

"I wasn't really naughty," said Pinkity. "The ink spilt by accident on the ribbon. I wouldn't have spoilt the dear Queen's ribbon for anything in the world."

"Well, you've been so kind to our ferns," said the fairies, "that we believe you. But how *did* you learn to be so clever, Pinkity?"

"I'm not clever *really*," said Pinkity, "but I can roll up ribbons nicely – it's the only thing I *can* do – so it was easy to roll up the ferns."

The fairies liked the shy little gnome, and took him in to breakfast with them. In the middle of it in walked Her Majesty the Queen!

"*Who* has looked after my baby ferns?" she asked in a pleased voice.

"Pinkity has! Pinkity has!" cried the fairies, pushing Pinkity forward. Then they told the Queen all about him.

"It was quite an accident that your lovely ribbon was spoilt," said Pinkity, "and I was dreadfully sorry, your Majesty."

"I'm quite *sure* it was an accident," said the Queen kindly, "and I have found out that all Mother Ribbony Rose cares about is gold, so I am sending her right away from Fairyland, and you need never go back!"

"Oh, how lovely!" cried Pinkity joyfully.

"Your Majesty! Let him look after the ferns and bracken, and teach other fairies how to roll up the baby ones!" begged the fairies. "He *is* so clever at it."

"Will you do that for us, Pinkity?" said the Queen.

"Oh, your Majesty, I would *love* it!" answered Pinkity joyfully, feeling happier than he had ever been in his life before.

He began his work that very day, and always now you will find that fern fronds are rolled up as tight as can be, just like the ribbon Pinkity rolled up at the ribbon shop.

As for old Mother Ribbony Rose, she was driven right away from Fairyland, and sent to live in the Land of Deep Regrets, and nobody has ever heard of her since.

Fiddle-de-dee, the Foolish Brownie

FIDDLE-DE-DEE was a young brownie. He lived with his mother in Pudding Cottage, and was very lazy indeed. He simply wouldn't do a thing, though his mother had far more than she could do.

"Now look here, Fiddle-de-dee," she said one day. "You really must help me. Your aunt and uncle are coming to tea, and I want some nice fresh muffins. You must go to the baker's and buy twelve."

So Fiddle-de-dee set off. He bought twelve muffins at the baker's and then started off home. On the way back he felt tired, so he jumped into a bus. At the next stop so many people got in that some had to stand.

"May I sit on your knee?" another brownie asked Fiddle-de-dee.

"Certainly," said Fiddle-de-dee – but he had the bag of muffins on his knee, and he wondered what to do with them. He slipped them underneath him, and then pulled the brownie down on to his knee. When the end of the ride came, the other brownie thanked him and they both got off the bus. The bag of muffins looked very strange.

How cross Fiddle-de-dee's mother was when she saw them!

"You stupid, silly fellow!" she cried. "You've been sitting on them!"

"Well, I had to put them somewhere," said Fiddle-de-dee. "If *I* hadn't sat on them the other brownie would have, for he sat on my knee. And as he was a lot heavier than I am, I thought it would be better if *I* sat on them!"

"You didn't think that you were *both* sitting on them, then?" asked his mother. "Now, listen, Fiddle-de-dee – the next time I send you out you must think what you're doing. You should have asked the baker to lend you a tray, and walked home with the muffins on your head like the muffin man."

"I see," said Fiddle-de-dee, and determined to do better next time.

Now two days later his mother thought it would be nice to have some ice-cream, for the day was hot. So she gave Fiddle-de-dee some money and told him to fetch some from the ice-cream shop. He set off, and bought a nice lot. It was in a cardboard box. He had just left the shop when he remembered how he had been scolded about the muffins.

"Mother said I ought to have brought them home on my head," he said.

"Well, I forgot to borrow a tray this time, but I'm sure I can balance this box on my head all right."

So he popped the box of ice-cream on his head, and walked home with it. But the sun was tremendously hot that day and beat down on Fiddle-de-dee all the way home. The ice-cream soon melted and began to run out of the corners of the box. It ran down Fiddle-de-dee's hair and trickled down his neck.

"Ooh!" said Fiddle-de-dee in surprise. "I do feel nice and cold. It isn't such a hot day after all. I'm not nearly so hot now."

The ice-cream went on trickling down his head and neck all the way home. When his mother saw him she gave a cry of dismay.

"Fiddle-de-dee!" she cried. "Whatever are you doing with the ice-cream, carrying it on your head like that in the hot sun! Oh, how foolish you are! It is all melted now, and you are in a terrible mess! You should have wrapped a damp cloth round the box, and covered it with your coat to keep it cool."

"Oh," said Fiddle-de-dee. "Well, how was I to know that? I'll do better next time."

The next day his mother heard that a fine goose was for sale, and she determined to buy it and keep it for Christmas-time.

"I'll fatten it up," she said, "and when Christmas comes it will make us a good Christmas dinner."

So she sent Fiddle-de-dee to get it. He bought it from the farmer, and set off with the goose. But he hadn't gone very far before he remembered how his mother had scolded him about the ice-cream.

"She said I ought to have wrapped it in a damp cloth and carried it home under my coat," he said. "Well, I must try to take the goose home as she said."

Hanging on a near-by clothes-line was a tablecloth belonging to Mother Wimple. Fiddle-de-dee took it down and soaked it in a pond. Then he wrapped the struggling, angry goose in it, and tried to put it under his coat. But the bird was big and strong, and it was all Fiddle-de-dee could do to hold it.

By the time he reached home his coat and shirt were rent and torn by the goose in its struggles to escape. The tablecloth was in rags, and Fiddle-de-dee was all hot and bothered.

"Oh my, oh my!" groaned his mother, when she saw him. "What *have* you been doing with Mother Wimple's lovely new tablecloth? And just look at your clothes, Fiddle-de-dee! They're only fit for the dustbin now! And the poor goose is half dead with fright!"

"I tried to do as you said," said Fiddle-de-dee, "but the goose didn't like being wrapped up in a damp cloth, Mother."

"You stupid, foolish boy," said his mother. "Can't a goose walk? You should have tied a string round its leg and let it follow behind you!"

"I see," said Fiddle-de-dee, and made up his mind to do better next time.
A week later his mother wanted him to fetch the joint of meat from the butcher's, so he set off. He took the leg of mutton from the man, and turned to go home. Then he remembered how angry his mother had been with him last time he had gone on an errand for her, and he tried to think how he should take the meat home.

"Mother said last time I ought to have tied a string to the goose's leg and let it follow behind me!" he thought. "Well, this mutton's got a leg, so I'll tie some string to it."

He found a piece of string in his pocket and carefully tied it to the leg of mutton. Then he threw it behind him, and set off home, dragging the meat after him.

He hadn't gone far when half the dogs and cats in the neighbourhood smelt the meat and came running after it. Fiddle-de-dee turned round and saw them all. He became frightened and started to run. All the dogs and cats ran too!

He tore home, the meat bumping up and down behind him. He raced in through the kitchen door – and all the cats and dogs came too, snarling, growling and fighting over the leg of mutton!

"Oh, good gracious, oh, my goodness!" cried his mother. "Whatever will you do next? What made you bring these creatures home with you? Look at that meat! You surely haven't dragged it home on a piece of string!"

"Well, that's what you told me to do with the goose," said Fiddle-de-dee.

"Yes, but a leg of mutton isn't a goose!" cried his mother, in a temper, and she boxed Fiddle-de-dee's ears. Then she picked up a broom, and shooed the dogs and cats away.

"Shoo, shoo, shoo!" she shouted. "Shoo, you cats, shoo, you dogs!"

When all the animals had gone away she turned to scold Fiddle-de-dee – but he wasn't there. He had gone to put himself to bed! He thought that would be the safest place for him that day, and he was quite right!

A Tin of Yellow Polish

Everyone would have liked Dame Round-Face very much if only she hadn't been such a borrower. She didn't borrow money – she borrowed things like brooms, lawn-mowers, a drop of milk, a pinch of tea. And she hardly ever paid for what she borrowed, or gave anything back in return.

The people in Snowdrop Village were generous and kind, and they didn't mind lending anything, but they did get tired of seeing Dame Round-Face popping her head in at their kitchen doors and hearing her say:

"*Have* you got a bit of soap you could lend me? I've run out of mine, and the shops are shut and I simply *must* finish my washing!"

If no one was in when Dame Round-Face called, she would just go in and help herself to what she wanted, and that made people very cross.

"What are we to do about it?" they said to one another. "We can't let Dame Round-Face go on behaving like this. It's bad for her, and makes us feel very cross."

But they couldn't do anything about it because Dame Round-Face didn't take any notice of them when they spoke to her about her bad habit.

"Oh, I'll pay it back all right," she would say, but she hardly ever did.

Now one day she wanted some polish to rub up her kitchen taps and her door-handles. She had none in her tin. It was quite empty! What a nuisance!

"Never mind – I'll borrow some from Mother Twinkle," thought Dame Round-Face, and off she went. But Mother Twinkle was out. Dame Round-Face tried the kitchen-door. It opened.

"Good!" thought Dame Round-Face. "I'll just pop in, get Mother Twinkle's polish, and slip back with it. She won't mind, I'm sure!"

She opened the cupboard door, and looked on the shelves, to see where Mother Twinkle kept her polish, and suddenly her eye caught sight of a tall, thin tin, bright yellow in colour. Tied round the neck of the tin was a magic duster! Dame Round-Face knew it was a magic one, because it changed colour as she looked at it, a thing that magic dusters always do.

"My!" thought the old lady. "Now this *is* a bit of luck! Magic yellow polish – and a magic duster to polish with! My word!"

It certainly was a bit of luck. The duster was so full of magic that it was quite well able to work by itself, once the polish was tipped out of the tin on to it. It

would whisk off to the nearest tap or door-handle and polish away like anything. Dame Round-Face wouldn't need to rub at all – the duster would do it all!

She ran back to her own cottage with the tin and the duster, feeling very pleased. She tipped out some of the yellow polish on to the duster, and then shook it out into the air. It flew off by itself at once, and settled on to the taps over the sink.

"Look at it polishing them!" said Dame Round-Face in delight. "My goodness me, those taps of mine will shine like the sun!"

They did. They shone so brightly that they seemed like lanterns in the dark corner over the sink. The duster whisked itself about a little and then flew to the door-handles. It began to polish away hard.

"You do the cupboard handles for me too," said Dame Round-Face, settling herself down in her rocking-chair. "I'm going to have a little sleep."

The duster polished all the door-handles and all the cupboard handles. Then it looked around for something else to polish. It saw two brass candlesticks on the mantelpiece and flew off to polish those, first getting itself a little more of the yellow polish out of the tall yellow tin.

When the candlesticks were done the duster couldn't find any more brass to polish. The doors were shut so it couldn't go into any other room to do some polishing there. It felt sad. It went over to Dame Round-Face, but she was fast asleep, and her mouth was wide open. Her face shone red.

The duster bent itself gently forward, made itself a point out of one of its corners, and carefully polished Dame Round-Face's front teeth. Soon they were a bright, shining yellow. The duster was pleased.

It started on Dame Round-Face's nose next. It polished it very, very gently so that she might not wake. The duster had never polished anyone's face before, and it couldn't help enjoying it.

It polished the old dame's nose till it was as bright yellow as the candlesticks. Then it polished her big ears. Then her cheeks, chin and forehead. It polished away and was quite sorry when it had finished.

It was tired at last and sank beside the tin on the table. After a while Dame Round-Face woke up. She rubbed her eyes, yawned, and looked round the room. How the taps, door-handles and candlesticks shone and twinkled!

"Marvellous!" said Dame Round-Face, very pleased. "I'd better take the polish and the duster back. If Mother Twinkle isn't home yet, she will never know I've borrowed it!"

Mother Twinkle wasn't home. Dame Round-Face popped the polish back on the shelf, with the duster. She shut the door and hurried home.

"I shan't tell Mother Twinkle I borrowed the duster and polish," she thought. "She might be rather cross, as they are magic ones."

But Mother Twinkle knew as soon as she opened her cupboard door that someone had borrowed her magic yellow polish and duster! For one thing, the duster was dirty, and for another thing the tin was half empty!

"Now, there's a mean trick to play on anyone!" said Mother Twinkle, crossly. "To come in while I am out, borrow my things without asking, and put them back without so much as waiting to say thank you! I guess it was old Dame Round-Face! I wish I could punish her. But she is sure to say she didn't borrow anything."

But Mother Twinkle didn't need to punish Dame Round-Face! She was being dreadfully punished, because of the shining yellow polish on her face and ears! When she went out that afternoon, without looking in her mirror first, she couldn't *think* why people stared at her so hard, and then turned away and laughed!

"She's got a yellow nose!" whispered little Jinky and Lobbo.

"Her ears are shining gold!" giggled Pitapat.

"Her teeth are yellow when she smiles!" laughed Clicky the pixie.

Dame Round-Face hurried home to look in the mirror to see what everyone was staring at. There she saw her shining, gleaming yellow face, with highly polished yellow ears! Oh, how dreadful, how dreadful!

"That tiresome duster must have polished me too!" cried Dame Round-Face. "Oh my, oh my! Now I must go to Mother Twinkle and ask her to take away this dreadful yellow-spell."

How Mother Twinkle laughed when she saw the shining, round, yellow face appearing round her kitchen door.

"Oh, Mother Twinkle, please take away the yellow-spell!" begged Dame Round-Face. "I simply can't bear it. Everyone is laughing at me."

"You deserve it," said Mother Twinkle, beginning to laugh again herself. "I shan't take the spell away. Keep it on your face to remind you not to borrow! It will wear away gradually as you wash each morning and night.

"And listen to me – although it will slowly fade, Dame Round-Face, it will become yellower again if you borrow anything!" said Mother Twinkle.

Poor Dame Round-Face! The yellow did slowly go away – but it always comes back again if she forgets and begins to borrow anything.

The Three Strange Travellers

ONCE upon a time there was a billy-goat who drew a little goat-carriage on the sea-sands. He took children quite a long ride on the beach. But one day, when he was getting old, he became lame. He limped with his right front hoof, and he could no longer draw the goat-carriage along at a fine pace.

"You are no use to me now," said his master, a cross and selfish old man. "I shall buy a new goat."

The old billy-goat bleated sadly. What would he do if his master no longer needed him?

"You can go loose on the common," said the old man. "Don't come to me for a home, for I don't want you any longer."

Poor Billy-goat! He was very unhappy. He looked at his little goat-carriage for the last time, and then he limped off to the common. The winter was coming on, and he hoped he would not freeze to death. He had always lived in a cosy shed in the winter-time – but now he would have no home.

He hadn't gone very far across the common when he heard a loud quacking behind him.

"Quack! Stop, I say! Hey, stop a minute! Quack!"

Billy-goat turned round. He saw a duck waddling along as fast as it could, quacking loudly.

"What's the matter?" asked Billy.

"Matter enough!" said the duck, quite out of breath. "Do you mind if I walk with you? There are people after me who will kill me if they find me."

"Mercy on us!" said the goat, startled. "Why do they want to kill you?"

"Well," said the duck indignantly, "I don't lay as many eggs as I did, and my master says I'm no use now, so he wants to eat me for his dinner. And I have served him well for many many months, laying delicious eggs, far nicer than any hen's!"

"Dear me," said Billy-goat, "you and I seem to have the same kind of master. Maybe they are brothers. Well, Duck, walk with me. I am seeking my fortune, and would be glad of company."

The two walked on together, the goat limping and the duck waddling. When they reached the end of the common they came to a farm.

"Do not go too near," said the duck. "I don't wish to be caught. Do you?" "No," said the goat. "Listen! What's that?"

They stood still and heard a great barking. Suddenly a little dog squeezed itself under a near-by gate and came running towards them. The duck hid behind the goat in fright, and the goat stood with his horns lowered in case the dog should attack him.

"Don't be afraid of me," panted the dog. "I am running away. My master has beaten me because I let a fox get two chickens last night. But what could I do? I was chained up and I could not get at the fox. I barked loudly, but my master was too fast asleep to hear me. And now he blames me for the fox's theft!"

"You are to be pitied," said the goat. "We too have had bad masters. Come with us, and we will keep together and look after ourselves. Maybe we shall find better masters."

"I will come," said the dog. "I am getting old, you know, and I cannot see as well as I used to do. I think my master wants to get rid of me and have a younger dog. Ah me, there is no kindness in the world these days!"

The three animals journeyed on together. They ate what they could find. The billy-goat munched the green grass, the duck swam on each pond she came to and hunted about for food in the mud at the bottom. The dog sometimes found a bit of bread or a hunk of meat thrown by the wayside.

They walked for miles and miles. Often the goat and the dog gave the duck rides on their backs, for she waddled so slowly, and soon got tired. At night they found a sheltered place beneath a bush, or beside a haystack, and slept there in a heap, the duck safely in the middle.

They became very fond of one another, and vowed that they would never separate. But as the days grew colder the three creatures became anxious.

"When the ponds are frozen I shall find no food," said the duck.

"And I shall not be able to eat grass when the ground is covered with snow," said the goat. "I shall freeze to death at night, for I have always been used to a shed in the winter."

"And I have been used to a warm kennel," said the dog. "What shall we do?"

They could think of no plan, so they wandered on. Then one afternoon a great storm blew up. Oh, my, what a wind! The snow came down softly everywhere, but the blizzard was so strong that even the soft snowflakes stung the dog's eyes and made the duck and the goat blink.

"We shall be lost altogether in this dreadful storm!" barked the dog. "We must find shelter."

The goat and the duck followed him. He put his nose to the ground and ran off. He went up a little hill, and at last came to a small cottage. There was a light in one of the windows.

"Somebody lives here," said the dog. "Let us knock at the door and ask for shelter."

So the goat tapped the door with his hoof. He bleated as he did so, the dog whined, and the duck quacked.

Inside the cottage was an old woman with a red shawl round her shoulders. She was darning a hole in a stocking and thinking about the dreadful storm. Suddenly she heard the tap-tap-tapping at her door.

"Bless us!" she cried, in a fright. "There's someone there! Shall I open the door or not? It may be a robber come through the storm to rob me of the gold pieces I have hidden so carefully in my old stocking under the mattress! No, I dare not open the door!"

As she sat trembling she heard the dog whining. Then she heard the bleating of the goat and the anxious quacking of the duck.

"Well, well!" she said in astonishment. "It sounds for all the world like a dog, a goat, and a duck! But how do they come to my door like this? Do they need shelter from this terrible storm, poor things? Well, I have no shed to put them in, so they must come in here with me."

She got up and went to the door. She undid the bolt and opened the door a crack. When she saw the trembling goat, the shivering dog, and the frightened duck, her kind heart melted at once and she opened the door wide.

"Poor lost creatures!" she said. "Come in, come in. You shall have warmth and shelter whilst this storm lasts. Then I've no doubt you will want to go back to your homes."

The three animals gladly came in to the warmth. The dog at once lay down on the hearth-rug, the goat stood near by, and the duck lay down in a corner, put her head under her wing and fell fast asleep, for she was very tired.

The old woman didn't know what to make of the three creatures. They seemed to know one another so well, and by the way they bleated, barked, and quacked to one another they could talk as well as she could.

The goat was very thin, and the dog was skinny too. As for the duck, when the old woman felt her, she was nothing but feathers and bone!

"The poor creatures!" said the kind old dame. "They are starving! I will give them a good meal to eat – they will feel all the better for it."

So she began to cook a meal of all the household scraps she had – bits of meat, vegetables, potatoes, bread, all sorts. How good it smelt! Even the duck in the corner stuck out her head from under her wing to have a good sniff.

The old woman took the big saucepan off the fire and stood it on the window-sill to cool. Then she ladled the warm food out into three dishes and put one in front of each animal.

"There, my dears," she said, "eat that and be happy tonight."

Well, the three animals could hardly believe their eyes to see such a feast! They gobbled up the food and left not a single scrap. Then the goat rubbed his head gently against the old dame's knee, the dog licked her hand, and the duck laid its head on her shoe. Then they call curled up in a heap together, and fell asleep. The old dame went to her bed and slept too.

In the morning the storm was over, but the countryside was covered with snow. The animals did not want to leave the warm cottage, but the old woman opened the door.

"Now you must find your way home," she said. She did not know that they had no homes. She thought they had lost their way in the storm, and that now they would be glad to go out and find their way back to their homes.

The animals were sad. They took leave of the kind woman, and wished they could tell her that they would like to stay; but she could not understand their language. They went out into the snow, and wondered where to go next.

"Let us go down the hill," said the goat. "See, there are some haystacks, and we may be able to find some food and shelter under the stacks to-night."

So down the hill they went. But they could not find any food. They crouched under the haystack that evening, and tried to get warm. As they lay there, quite still, they heard the sound of soft footsteps in the snow. Then they heard voices.

"The old woman has a great hoard of gold," said one voice. "We will go to her cottage to-night, when she is in bed, and steal it."

"Very well," said the second voice. "I will meet you there, and we will share the gold. She has no dog to bark or bite."

The animals listened in horror. Why, it must be the kind old woman these horrid men were speaking of! How could they save her from the robbers?

"We must go back to the cottage," said the dog. "Somehow we must creep in and wait for these robbers. Then we will give them the fright of their lives!"

So the three limped, walked and waddled all the way up the hill until they came to the little cottage. The old woman was going to bed. The goat peeped in at the window and saw her blow her candle out.

"She has left this window a little bit open," he said to the dog. "Can you jump in and open the door for me and the duck?"

"Yes," said the dog, "I can do that. I often saw my master open the farm doors. I know how to do it."

He squeezed in through the window and went to the door. He pulled at the latch. The door was not bolted, so the goat and the duck came in at once. They could hear the old dame snoring.

"What shall we do when the robbers come?" asked the duck excitedly.

"I have a plan," said the goat. "You, duck, shall first of all frighten the robbers by quacking at the top of your very loud voice. You, dog, shall fly at the legs of the first robber, and I will lower my head and butt the second one right in the middle. Ha! what a fright we will give them!"

The three animals were so excited that they could hardly keep still. The duck flew up on the table and stood there. The dog hid behind the door. The goat stood ready on the hearth-rug, for he wanted a good run when he butted the second robber.

Presently the dog's sharp ears told him that the two robbers were outside. He warned the others and they got ready to do their parts. The robbers pushed the door open.

At that moment the duck opened her beak and quacked. How she quacked! QUACK! QUACK! QUACK! QUACK! QUACK!

Then the dog flew at the legs of the first robber and bit them And he growled. GRRRRRRRRRRRR! What a terrible growl it was!

Then the goat ran at the second robber and butted him so hard in the middle that he sat down suddenly and lost all his breath.

The duck was so excited that she wanted to join in the fun. So she flew to the robbers and pecked their noses hard. PECK! PECK!

The robbers were frightened almost out of their lives. They couldn't think what was happening! There was such a terrible noise going on, and something was biting, hitting and pecking them from top to toe. How they wished they had never come near the cottage!

As soon as they could they got to their feet and ran. The duck flew after them and pecked their ankles. The dog tore pieces out of their trousers. The goat limped as fast as he could and butted them down the hill. My, what a set-to it was!

The two robbers fell into a ditch and covered themselves with mud.

"That old woman is a witch!" cried one.

"Yes, she pinched my ears!" said the other. "And she bit my legs!"

"Ho, and she punched me in the middle so that I lost all my breath!" said the first.

"And all the time she made such a noise!" cried the second, trying to clamber out of the ditch. "She said: 'Whack! Whack! Whack!'"

"Yes, and she cried: 'Cuff! Cuff! Cuff!' too!" said the first. "And how she chased us down the hill!" The three animals laughed till the tears came into their eyes when they heard the robbers talking like this.

"They thought my 'Quack, quack, quack!' was 'Whack, whack, whack!'" said the duck in delight.

"And they thought my 'Wuff, wuff, wuff!' was 'Cuff, cuff, cuff!'" said the dog, jumping about joyfully. "What a joke! How we frightened them!"

"Let us go back and see if the old dame is all right," said the goat. "She woke when the duck began to quack."

Back they all went to the cottage, and found the old dame sitting up in bed, trembling, with a candle lighted by her side. When she saw the three animals she could hardly believe her eyes.

"So it was you who set upon those robbers and chased them away!" she said. "You dear, kind, clever creatures! Why, I thought you had gone to your homes!"

The goat went up to the bed and put his front paws there. The dog put his nose on the quilt. The duck flew up on the bed-rail and flapped her wings.

"Wuff!" said the dog, meaning: "We want to stay with you!"

"Bleat!" said the goat, and meant the same thing.

"Quack!" said the duck, and she meant the same thing too.

And this time the old dame understood them, and she smiled joyfully.

"So you want to stay here?" she said. "Well, you shall. I'm all alone and I want company. It's wintertime and I expect you need shelter, so you shall all live with me. I shall always be grateful to you for chasing away those robbers."

Well, those three animals soon settled down with the old woman. The duck laid an egg for her breakfast each day. The dog lay on the door-mat and guarded the cottage for her each night. The goat was troubled because he could do nothing for his kind mistress.

But one day he found how well he could help her. She had to go to the woods to get firewood. She took with her a little cart to bring it back, and this she had to pull herself, for she had no pony.

But the goat stood himself in the shafts and bleated. The old woman saw that he wanted her to tie the cart to him so that he might pull the wood home for her, and she was delighted. Every day after that the goat took the cart to the woods for his mistress, and very happy they were together.

As for the robbers, they have never dared to come back. They went a hundred miles away, and told the people there a marvellous story of an old witch who cried: "Whack! Cuff! Whack! Cuff!" and could bite, pinch, and punch all at once. But nobody believed them.

The old dame and the dog, goat, and duck still live together very happily. Their house is called "Windy Cottage," so if ever you pass by, go in and see them all. The old dame will love to tell you the story of how they came to live together!

The Invisible Gnome

THERE was once a gnome called Too-Much. He was called Too-Much because he was very fat, so there was too much of him. He was very greedy, very sly, and not at all to be trusted.

Now one day he stole a hat belonging to a witch. When he put it on – hey presto, he couldn't be seen! Marvellous! The hat was rather small, but that didn't matter – as soon as he wore it Too-Much disappeared – and then, think of the tricks he could get up to!

"I'll use this hat to get myself as many cakes, pies, and apples as I like," thought Too-Much gleefully. "My word, what a time I'll have!"

He clapped on the hat and went off down the street. Nobody could see him. How he chuckled! He went to Dame Biscuit's cake-shop and looked in at the window.

"Currant buns! Doughnuts with jam! Gingerbread fingers! Oooooh! Here I go!" And into the shop he went. His quick fingers took three currant buns, two doughnuts, and six gingerbread fingers. Then out he went. Dame Biscuit was most amazed when she saw the cakes disappearing, and she cried out in rage.

"Hi! Come back, cakes!" She could see them travelling through the air, but she couldn't see who was taking them!

But of course the cakes didn't come back. They soon disappeared down Too-Much's throat. Then he went to the pie-shop, and Mister Crusty saw, to his great surprise, three large pies rise into the air and go out of the door. He took a stick and ran after them – but it wasn't long before they went the same way as the cakes.

"This is fine!" said Too-Much in delight. "What a splendid way of getting what I want! Now for a drink!"

He stopped outside the lemonade-shop and looked into the window. Then in he went and took a glass from the counter. The shopkeeper shouted in fear when he saw the glass dipping itself into the jar of lemonade. It came out full, tilted itself up, and out fell the lemonade – and disappeared entirely!

"Oooh! Magic! Bad Magic!" yelled the shopkeeper, and ran out into the street, calling people to come and see. But Too-Much slipped out with him and went towards the market-place.

He didn't want anything more to eat and drink for a while, so he amused himself by taking all the farmers' hats off, one by one, and throwing them into the horse-trough.

What an uproar there was in the market! Soon there was a fight going on, for each farmer thought another had knocked off his hat.

Suddenly a bell rang, and everyone stood still. On the steps of the Town Hall stood Bron, the chief gnome of the town.

"What's all this?" he roared. "You should be ashamed of yourselves."

Too-Much skipped up the steps unseen, took off the chief gnome's hat, and threw it neatly on to the roof of the Town Hall. Bron gaped in astonishment, and everyone roared with laughter.

"It's an invisible gnome!" cried the farmers. "We shall have to catch him, or he will plague the life out of us."

But how? Ah, that was the question.

Too-Much, still wearing the witch-hat, stole sweets, pears, and apples next. Soon the whole town wanted to catch him – and once they very nearly did. Too-Much trod in a puddle – and suddenly the marks of wet feet appeared on the pavement, though there seemed to be nobody walking there.

"There he is!" cried everyone, and ran after the trail of wet foot-marks. Too-Much, glancing round, saw the townsfolk after him and ran for his life. He tore into the nearest house, which happened to be Mother Twitchet's, and found himself in her parlour. The townsfolk rushed after him, much to Mother Twitchet's surprise and anger, for she was having a nap.

"Shut all the doors," cried Bron, the chief gnome. "He's in here somewhere."

So all the doors were shut. Then Bron made everyone sit down on the floor whilst he went round the room, his hands stretched out as if he were playing Blind Man's Buff. But Too-Much found it easy to slip away, for he could see Bron all the time.

"What are we to do?" groaned Bron. "Someone else try now!"

So the others tried to find Too-Much, but no one could. By this time it was evening, and Mother Twitchet said they must go and leave her in peace.

"But that sly gnome is somewhere about your parlour," said Bron. "You don't want him here all night, do you, snoozing by your fire?"

"Don't you worry – *I* can find him all right," said Dame Twitchet. "You come here in the morning, Bron, and you'll find I've got him for you. It takes a cleverer gnome than this invisible one to get the better of old Mother Twitchet."

"You boast too much," said Bron crossly. "See you keep your word, or I'll have something to say to you to-morrow."

He held the door a very little open, and all the gnomes slipped out. Bron made sure that the invisible gnome did not slip out too, then he went. The door was locked on the outside, and Mother Twitchet was left alone.

"Are you going to show yourself, or shall I make you?" said Mother Twitchet. Too-Much said nothing, but just grinned to himself. Mother Twitchet went to a drawer and took out a little yellow box full of sneezing powder. It was a favourite snuff of hers, very strong indeed. She first wrapped a handkerchief round her nose so that she would not smell it herself, then she took pinches of the powder between finger and thumb and scattered them all over the room.

Too-Much was hiding behind the sofa. As soon as a pinch of snuff flew there, it tickled his nose terribly. He got out his handkerchief and buried his face in it – but the mischief was done.

'A-TISHOO!" he said. "A-TISHOO! A-TISHOO!"

His head jerked as he sneezed, and off flew his tight witch-hat. Mother Twitchet ran to the sofa as soon as she heard the first sneeze and snatched up the fallen hat. Then she dragged Too-Much out – and, my word, the spanking she gave him! How he howled! How he yelled!

She tied him up to her mangle – and there he was next day when Bron peeped in at the door. Oh, clever Mother Twitchet!

Father Time and His Pattern Book

One New Year's Eve, in the middle of the night, Robin woke up with a jump. He sat up in bed and listened. Whatever could have awakened him?

Then he heard slow footsteps outside his window, and he wondered who could be wandering round the garden in the middle of the night!

"Perhaps it is someone lost in the snow," he thought. So he jumped out of bed and went to the window. He opened it and leaned out. It was dark outside, but he could just make out something moving below.

"Who's there?" he called. And a most surprising answer came up to him:

"I'm Old Father Time! I've come to collect this year's patterns."

"This year's patterns! Whatever do you mean?" said Robin in astonishment. "And what are you doing in our garden?"

"Well, I came to collect your pattern too," said the old man.

"I haven't got a pattern!" said Robin. "You must be dreaming."

"Maybe I am," said Father Time. "But my dreams are true ones. It's cold out here, little boy. Let me in and I will show you some of my patterns."

"I think there's a fire in the dining-room, if it hasn't quite gone out," said Robin, excited. "I'll let you in at the front door, and we can go into the dining-room for a bit. Shall I wake Mother?"

"Oh no," said Father Time. "Don't wake anyone. Hurry up and let me in."

Robin slipped downstairs. He opened the front door quietly and someone came in. Robin went to the dining-room and switched on the light. Then he saw his visitor for the first time.

Father Time was an old, old man. His beard almost reached the ground. He had a wise and kindly face, with dreamy, happy eyes and a sad mouth. He carried a great scythe with him, which Robin was most surprised to see.

"What's that for?" he asked. "Did you get it out of our gardener's shed? It's what we use to cut the long grass."

"This scythe is mine," said Father Time. "I use it to cut away the years from one another. I cut time with it."

"How strange!" said Robin, feeling excited. "Now, do show me the patterns you spoke about! Where are they? And what are they?"

Father Time didn't have any book of patterns. Robin had thought he would have one rather like the book of patterns that Mother sometimes got from the man who sold them their curtains. But except for his scythe he had nothing at all.

"My patterns?" he said. "Oh, I have them all, though you can't see them just at the moment. Every one makes a pattern of his life, you know. Your brother does. Your friends do. You do. I'll show you any pattern you like to ask me for."

"Well – I'd like to see what pattern my brother made last year," said Robin.

Father Time put down his scythe carefully. He put out the light. Then he held up his hands in the darkness and from the fingers of Old Father Time there flowed a shining ribbon, broad and quivering as if it were alive. It was as wide as the table, and it flowed down on to it like a cloth, spreading itself flat for Robin to see.

"I say! It's a lovely pattern," said Robin. "I shouldn't have thought my little brother could have made such a beauty. How did he make it?"

"The pattern is made of the stuff he put into each day," said Father Time. "The happy moments – the times he ran to do a kindness – the times he cried with fear or pain. They are all in the pattern. This line of silver is a line of love – he loves very much – for it is a beautiful line. This glowing thread shows his happy times – he is a happy little boy. This shimmering piece is a great kindness he did, about the middle of the year. It shines because it still shines in every one's memory."

"Yes – I remember that," said Robin. "I hurt my leg and couldn't go to a party. So Lennie wouldn't go either, and he brought me every single one of his toys and gave me them for my own, because he was so sorry for me – even his best railway train that he loves. I shall never forget how kind he was to me. But what is this ugly little line of black dots that keeps showing in the pattern?"

"Those spots come into a pattern when the maker of the pattern loses his temper," said Father Time. "He must be careful, or as the years go on the spots will get bigger and bigger and spoil his pattern altogether."

"Oh dear – I'll have to warn him," said Robin. "Now show me Harry's pattern, Father Time. You know – Harry Jones. He lives next door. Have you got his for last year?"

"Yes, I collected it tonight," said Father Time. The pattern he had been showing Robin faded away into the darkness, and from Father Time's fingers flowed another one that spread itself on the table as the other had done.

It was an ugly pattern, with two or three bright threads lighting it up. Robin looked at it.

"It's not a very beautiful pattern, is it?" he asked.

"No. Harry cannot have done well with his three hundred and sixty-five days last year," said Father Time sadly. "See – that horrid mess there means greediness and selfishness – and here it is again – and again – spoiling the pattern that the bright threads are trying to make."

"Yes – Harry *is* selfish," said Robin. "He's an only child, and thinks everything must be for him. What are the bright threads, Father Time?"

Father Time looked at them closely. "They are fine strong bits of pattern," he said. "They are the hard work that Harry has done. He is a good worker, and if he goes on trying hard, those bright threads will be so strong that they will run right through those messy bits. Maybe one day he will make a better pattern."

The pattern faded. Robin thought for a moment, and then he asked for another. "Show me Elsie's, please," he said. "She's such a nice girl. I like her."

Once again a pattern flowed over the table. It was a brilliant one, beautiful and even. It would have been quite perfect except that it seemed to be torn here and there.

"It's lovely except for those torn bits," said Robin.

"Yes – Elsie must be a happy and clever girl," said Father Time. "But alas – look at these places where the pattern is quite spoilt! That means cruelty, Robin – a thing that tears the pattern of our lives to bits. Poor Elsie! She must be careful, or one day her pattern will be torn to pieces, and all her happiness will go."

"How strange, Father Time!" said Robin, astonished. "That's the one thing I can't bear about Elsie – she is so unkind to animals. I've often seen her throw stones at them. And yet she's so nice in every other way."

"Tell her about her pattern," said Father Time. "For maybe one day a moment of cruelty will spoil a whole year or more."

"Now show me Leslie's pattern," said Robin. "He's such a funny little boy, Father Time – so shy and timid, like a mouse! I'd love to see the kind of pattern that he has made this last year."

Once again a pattern flowed in the darkness – but what a strange one! It could hardly be seen. There was no brightness in it, no real pattern to see. It was just a smudge of dingy colours.

"Poor little boy!" said Father Time. "He is afraid of everything! He has put no brightness into his pattern, no happy moments, no kindness – only shyness and fear. Robin, you must help him to make a better pattern next year. Tell him to have courage and not to be afraid of doing kindness to anyone – then his pattern will glow and shine."

The pattern faded. Father Time went to switch on the light. "I must go," he said. "I have many other patterns to collect tonight, and to put into my book of history."

"Wait a minute!" said Robin. "Please, Father Time – may I see my own pattern?"

"Yes, you may," said Father Time. He didn't put on the light but held up his strange fingers once again. And from them flowed the pattern of all the days of the last year – the pattern made by Robin himself.

Robin looked at it, half fearful, half excited, wondering what he would see. He saw a brilliant pattern, full of bright colours that danced and shone. In it were pools of silver light, but here and there were smudges of grey that spoilt the lovely pattern he had made.

"Ah, Robin, you have done well this year to make such a fine pattern," said Father Time, pleased. "You have been happy, for see how the pattern glows. You have worked hard, for see how strong the pattern is, unbroken and steady. You have been kind, for here are the silver pools that shine in the pattern and shine in your friends' memories, too."

"But, Father Time – what are those grey smudges that spoil the pattern here and there?" asked Robin, puzzled. "I don't like them."

"Neither do I," said Father time. "They show where you spoilt your days by telling lies, Robin. Truth always shines out in a pattern, but lies smudge it with grey. See – you did not tell the truth there – and there – and there – and look, as the pattern reaches the end of the year, the grey smudges got worse. You have let that bad habit grow on you and spoil the lovely pattern you were making."

"Yes," said Robin, ashamed. "I have been getting worse about telling lies, I know. Mother keeps telling me that. I didn't know that they would spoil the pattern of my year, though. I'll be very, very careful next year – I shan't tell a single lie, then my pattern will be really lovely."

"Be careful nothing else creeps in to spoil it," said Father Time. "I will come next year and show you the pattern you have made. Now good-bye – I must go. I feel much warmer and I have enjoyed our talk!"

"So have I! It was wonderful," asaid Robin. "Thank you very much, Father Time!"

The old man slipped out of the house and Robin went back to bed. He dreamed all night long of the year's patterns, and when he awoke in the morning he couldn't think whether it had *all* been a dream or not.

"Anyway, I shall know next New Year's Eve," said Robin. "I shall look out for the old man again then – and see the pattern I have made! I do hope it's beautiful."

Would you like to see the one you made last year? What do you think it would be like? I *would* love to know!

Old Bufo the Toad

OLD BUFO was a toad, fat, brown and ugly. The only beautiful thing about him was his pair of bright, copper eyes. They were like two shining jewels.

Bufo was not allowed in Fairyland. The fairies said he really was much too ugly. He frightened them. So Bufo lived in our world, under a big stone by the stream. He had a little shop under his stone, and there he worked hard all day long.

What do you think he made? Guess! Yes – toadstools! He was very clever indeed at making these. First he would make a nice sturdy stump, then a pretty curved cap-like top, and then underneath he sewed dozens of tiny frills. So you can see he was a busy fellow.

Now one day the Queen of Fairyland went on a long journey. She visited the Moon. She visited the Land of Dreams. And she visited our world too. She went with six servants, and she wore no crown, for she did not want to be known as she passed here and there.

She called herself Dame Silverwings, and travelled about quite safely in her silver coach, drawn by two white mice.

One day she heard that someone was chasing after her coach to catch her. It was the wizard Tall-Hat. He had found out that Dame Silverwings was none other than the Fairy Queen herself, and he thought that it would be a fine thing to catch her and take her prisoner. He would not let her go until he had been paid ten sacks of gold. Aha! How rich he would be!

A blackbird warned the Queen that Tall-Hat was after her. She hurried on her way – and then alas! a fog came down – and she was lost! On and on went her little white mice, dragging the carriage, but they did not know at all where they were going. When the fog cleared, they were quite lost.

The Queen stepped from her carriage. She was by a stream in a wood. No one seemed to be about at all.

"Is anyone living near here?" she called in her bird-like voice. She listened for an answer – and one came. It was the voice of Bufo, the old toad, that answered. His home was under the big stone nearby. He crawled out and croaked loudly:

"Yes – I, Bufo the toad, live here. Pray come and shelter, if you wish."

The Queen and her six servants looked at Bufo in surprise, but when they saw his beautiful coppery eyes they trusted him and went to his stone. The Queen was surprised to see such a pretty and neat little shop under the stone – and when she saw the stools she was delighted.

"May I sit down on one of these dear little stools?" she asked. "Oh, how nice they are! Just the right height, too! I would like to rest here awhile."

"Then pray rest on my toadstools," said Bufo. "I have enough for all of you. And let me offer you each a glass of honey-dew."

The kindly old toad fussed over his visitors and made them very welcome. The Queen was glad to rest on the quaint toadstool after her long ride.

"I am Dame Silverwings," she said. "Which is the quickest way to Fairyland from here?"

"Do you see this stream?" said Bufo. "Well, on the other side lies Fairyland. There is a bridge a little farther on."

"Oh, we shall soon be home then," said the fairy, very pleased. But just as she said that she heard the noise of wings and, peeping from the stone, she saw to her horror the Tall-Hat Wizard himself, looking all round for her. He passed by, and she knew he had gone to the bridge to guard it so that she could not cross to Fairyland.

She began to weep. Bufo the toad could not bear to see her tears, and he begged her to tell him what was the matter. As soon as he heard about Tall-Hat guarding the bridge to Fairyland, he laughed.

"We can easily trick him," he said. "You shall cross the stream another way."

"But there are no boats here," said the Queen.

"I have something that will do just as well," said Bufo. He took up one of his

toadstools and turned it upside down. "Look," he said, "if I put this into the water upside down, you can sit on the little frills and hold on to the stalk, then the toadstool will float you across the stream safely. I have seven fine toadstools I can spare for you."

In the greatest delight the Queen and her servants hurried down to the water with the toadstools. They let them float there upside down. Then one by one they climbed on to their toadstools, waved good-bye to old Bufo, and floated to the opposite side. Once there they were safe!

Tall-Hat waited by the bridge for six weeks – and then heard that the Queen had been safely back in Fairyland all that time. How angry he was! And how Bufo the toad laughed when he heard him go by, shouting and raging! He didn't know that Bufo was peeping at him from under his big stone.

Bufo got such a surprise when he knew that the little fairy he had helped was the Fairy Queen herself. She sent him a gold watch and chain to wear, and an order for as many toadstools as he and his friends could make. "They will do so nicely for our parties in the woods," she said.

So now Bufo and his family make toadstools all day long, and stand them about in the woods for the little folk to sit on, or to use for tables at their parties. And Bufo is allowed in Fairyland, and has a grand time at the palace once a month when he goes to tea with the Queen herself. Nobody thinks he is ugly now, for they always look at his glowing eyes. Have you see them? You haven't? Well, just look at them next time you see an old toad hopping along.

And don't forget to look at the dear little frills Bufo puts under every toadstool, will you?

Well Done, Bob-Along!

WHENEVER anyone in Brownie Town had a party they always went shopping at Mr. Knobbly's shop. He was a brownie with bright green eyes and such bony hands and arms and legs that really Mr. Knobbly was a very good name for him.

"Everything for parties!" Mr. Knobbly would call out when any of the little folk went by. "Balloons of all colours, big and bouncy, blown up as large as you like. Funny hats for everyone – buy a bonnet for Mr. Grumble, buy a dunce's hat for the schoolmaster! Crackers to pull with the biggest BANG you ever heard!"

It was a lovely shop to wander round. Balloons bumped against your head, pretty lanterns swung to and fro, funny hats could be tried on, and shining ornaments glittered everywhere.

All the same nobody liked Mr. Knobbly very much. He was a cheat, and when anybody ordered two dozen balloons, he would send only twenty-two or twenty-three, and hope that nobody would bother to count them. And often some of his crackers had nothing in them, and that was very disappointing indeed.

One day Mr. Knobbly was very, very pleased. Mr. Popple, the richest brownie in the town, was giving a big party for his little girl, Peronel, and, of course, he had been to order a great many things from Mr. Knobbly's shop.

"I want one hundred balloons," he said. "And twelve boxes of crackers, each with a nice little present inside. And one hundred funny hats, with strong elastic for each one, so that the children can keep them on easily. I'll pay you well, so be sure to see that everything is first-class."

"Certainly, Mr. Popple, sir, certainly," said Mr. Knobbly, too delighted for words. "When is this party, sir?"

"In one week's time," said Mr. Popple. "All the balloons must be blown up very big, and have nice long strings, and be delivered on the morning of the party, so that they can be hung up all round the room."

Mr. Knobbly was soon very, very busy. He made a great many funny hats, and indeed he was very clever at that. But he wasn't going to put good strong elastic on them – oh no –

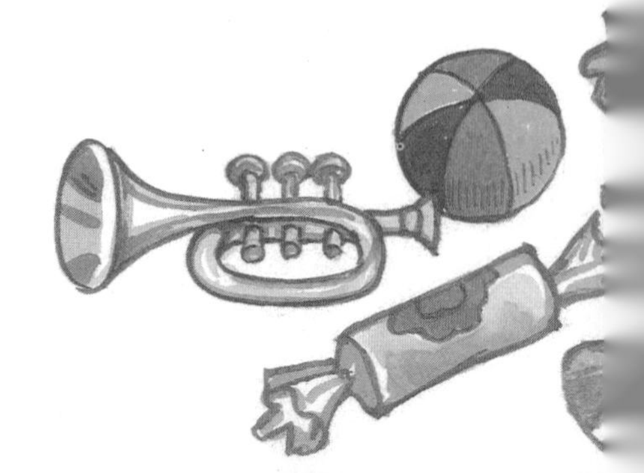

strong elastic was expensive – he would get very cheap stuff. Nobody would notice!

"And I'm not going to put presents into each cracker, either," said Mr. Knobbly to himself. "Often when a cracker is pulled, the present shoots out and goes under the table or somewhere! If a cracker has no present in it, the child will think it's flown right out and go to look for it. He won't know that he'll never find it because it wasn't there! Ha, ha – I'm a wily brownie, I am!" It was when he came to blow up the balloons that he found himself in difficulties.

He didn't mind blowing up a dozen, he had often done that – but a hundred! He looked at the piles of flat rubber, all balloons waiting to be blown up, and he shook his head.

"No – I can't do it. I'll have to get someone in to help." So he put a notice in his window.

WANTED
SOMEONE TO BLOW UP
BALLOONS

That day a small, rather raggedy brownie came by. He went about doing odd jobs, and he was a merry, honest little fellow that everybody liked. He saw the notice and popped his head round the door. "I can blow up balloons," he said. "I've plenty of very good breath, available at any moment of the day. I can also put a whistle into any balloon when I blow it up."

"What do you mean?" said Knobbly, surprised.

"Well, I whistle as I blow," said the brownie, "and naturally, when I fill a balloon with my breath and whistle at the same time, the whistle goes into the balloon too – and when it's going down, as balloons do sooner or later, it whistles to warn the owner to blow it up again!"

"How extraordinary!" said Knobbly, thinking that he could certainly charge extra for Whistling Balloons. "All right, you can have the job. What's your name?"

"Bob-Along," said the brownie. "And I'm as honest as the day, as anyone will tell you. What will you pay me?"

"Depends on your work," said Knobbly. "Now look – fasten elastic on these hats for me, before you begin on the balloons."

Bob-Along fixed elastic on a clown's hat and then popped it on. But the elastic broke at once.

"Hey," said Bob-Along, "this elastic's no good. Give me stronger pieces."

"You just do as you're told," said Knobbly, who was busy making crackers. Bob-Along picked one up. It was very pretty indeed. He shook it.

"Nothing inside!" he said, and took a toy and pushed it into the cracker.

"You stop that," said Knobbly crossly. "I'm doing the crackers!"

Bob-Along watched him. "Well, you're not doing them very well," he said, after a minute or two. "You've missed putting toys into two more crackers. Better let me put the toys in for you, while you make them."

"You blow up the balloons," said Knobbly, getting tired of being watched by this bright-eyed brownie. "Another word from you and I'll kick you out of my shop!"

"You won't," said Bob-Along. "You haven't any breath to blow up your balloons! I've plenty! I'll start on them now, whistle and all!"

Well, Bob-Along certainly did know how to blow up balloons steadily and well. He whistled as he blew, and showed Knobbly how his whistle came out of the balloon again when he let the air out of it. It was really very peculiar. Knobbly was pleased, and decided to charge even more for them than he had planned at first.

More and more balloons were blown up by Bob-Along, and he tied each one's neck with string, and hung it to a pole, so that it did not get entangled with the others. Soon there were thirty hanging up, bobbing about gaily.

"Shall I shake each cracker for you, and see if you've left out any toys?" asked Bob-Along. "I want a rest from blowing now. I never blow up more than thirty balloons at a time, in case I use up all my breath."

"Don't be silly," said Knobbly. "If you feel like that you can come back tomorrow – but they'll *have* to be finished then, because that's the day of the party."

Bob-Along finished all the balloons the next day, and then, as Knobbly asked him, took them to Mr. Popple's big house. Mr. Popple was very, very pleased with such big ones, especially when he knew that a whistle had been blown into each one. Then Bob-Along went back to Knobbly's.

"I want my money now, please," he said.

"Here you are – fourpence," said Knobbly, and threw the pennies on the table.

"What – fourpence for my excellent work!" cried Bob-Along.

"You'll take fourpence or nothing," said Knobbly, making the last cracker.

"Then I'll take nothing – except what I've put into your balloons!" said Bob-Along, and marched out.

"Hey – what do you mean?" cried Knobbly, but Bob-Along didn't answer. He went straight to Mr. Popple's and slipped into the party room, where the hundred balloons swung and swayed.

He untied the neck of first one and then another. The air came out with a loud whistle and the balloons went flat. Then Bob-Along undid three more, and again the air came out whistling. Mr. Popple heard the noise and came running in. "Look here – what are you doing?" he cried. "You've blown all those up – why are you making them flat again? You've been paid for that work!"

"No, I haven't," said Bob-Along. "Knobbly offered me fourpence, and I wouldn't take such a poor sum. So I've come to take away my breath – the breath I put into each balloon, and the whistle too. They're mine – my breath and my whistle – and if I'm not going to be paid for them, I'll have them back!"

"You dishonest fellow!" cried Mr. Popple.

"Oh no, I'm not!" said Bob-Along. "It's Mr. Knobbly who's dishonest! You ask him how many crackers he's *not* put toys into! You try on one of his funny hats and see how the elastic snaps at once. Well, he may trick *you* – but he's not going to trick *me*!"

"Wait!" said Mr. Popple. "Come down to Knobbly's with me. I'll soon get your money for you!" And away he went with Bob-Along grinning beside him. What a shock Mr. Knobbly had when they walked into his shop. Mr. Popple shook all the crackers and found that nine of them were empty! He tried on three funny hats and each time the elastic snapped almost at once.

"Ha! And you wouldn't pay a fair wage to this good worker here!" shouted Mr. Popple. "Wait till I get my wand! I'll wish you away to the darkest cave in the mountains, you dishonest brownie!"

But Mr. Knobbly didn't wait. He took to his heels and fled, and never came back again. And Bob-Along quickly put strong elastic on to the hats and filled the empty crackers, and blew up the flat balloons – *and* went to the party too!

And who do you suppose has Knobbly's shop now? Yes, little Bob-Along, with his merry face and honest ways. Well, he deserves to have it, doesn't he!

Do Hurry Up, Dinah!

ONCE upon a time there was a little girl called Dinah. She was pretty and had nice manners, and she was kind and generous.

But OH, how slow she was!

You should just have seen her dressing in the morning. She took about five minutes finding a sock. Then she took another five minutes putting it on. Then she spent another five minutes taking it off because it was inside out. By the time she was dressed and downstairs everyone else had finished breakfast.

At breakfast-time she was just as slow. You really would have laughed to see her eating her porridge. First she sat staring at her plate. Then she put the sugar on very, very slowly and very, very carefully. Then she put on her milk. She stirred the porridge slowly round and round and round, and then she began to eat it.

She took quite half an hour to eat it, so she was always late for school. And, dear me, when she did get to school what a time she took taking off her coat and hat. What a time she was getting out her pencil and rubber and book! By the time that Dinah was ready to begin her work the lesson was finished.

She had two names. One was Slow-coach, which her mother called her, and the other was Tortoise, which her teacher called her.

"Dinah, you should have been born a tortoise!" the teacher used to say. "You really should. You would have been quite happy as a slow old tortoise!"

"Well," said Dinah, "I wish I lived in Tortoise-town, wherever it is! I hate people always saying 'Do hurry up, Dinah; do hurry up, Dinah!' I'd *like* to live with tortoises. I'm sure they wouldn't keep hustling and bustling me like everyone else does."

Now it so happened that the wind changed at the very moment that Dinah said this. You know that many strange things are said to happen when the wind changes, don't you? Well, sometimes a wish will come true at the exact change of the wind – and that's what happened to Dinah!

Her wish came true. She suddenly found that everything round her went quite black, and she put out her hand to steady herself, for she felt giddy.

She caught hold of something and held on to it tightly. The blackness gradually faded, and Dinah blinked her eyes. She looked round, expecting to see the school-room and all the boys and girls sitting down writing.

But she didn't see that. She saw something most strange and peculiar – so peculiar that the little girl blinked her eyes in astonishment.

She was in a little village street! The sun shone down overhead, and around Dinah were funny little houses, with oval doors, instead of oblong ones like ours.

She was holding on to something that was beginning to get very angry. "Let go!" said a slow, deep voice. "What's the matter? Let go, I say! Do you want to pull my shell off my back!"

Then, to Dinah's enormous surprise, she saw that she was holding tightly on to a tortoise as big as herself! He was standing on his hind legs, and he wore a blue coat, short yellow trousers, and a blue hat on his funny little wrinkled head.

Dinah stared at him in amazement. "Who are you?" she asked.

"I'm Mr. Crawl," said the tortoise. "Will you let go, please?"

Dinah let go. She was so surprised and puzzled at finding herself in a strange village all of a sudden with a tortoise walking by, that she could hardly say a word. But at last she spoke again.

"Where am I?" she asked.

"In Tortoise-town," said the tortoise. "Dear me, *I* know you! You're the little girl that is called Tortoise at school, aren't you? You wanted to come here, didn't you – and here you are! Well, well – you'd better come home with me and my wife will look after you. Come along."

"I want to go home," said Dinah.

"You can't," said Mr. Crawl. "Here you are and here you'll stay. No doubt about that. You should be pleased that your wish came true. Dear, dear, don't go so quickly. I can't possibly keep up with you!"

Dinah wasn't really going quickly. She always walked very slowly indeed – but the old tortoise shuffled along at the rate of about an inch a minute!

"Do hurry up!" said Dinah at last. "I can't walk as slowly as this. I really can't."

"My dear child, you were called Tortoise at school, so you must be very, very slow," said Mr. Crawl. "Now, here we are at last. There's Mrs. Crawl at the door."

It was all very astonishing to Dinah. She had passed many tortoises in the road, some big, some small, all wearing clothes, and talking slowly to one another in their strange deep voices. Even the boy and girl tortoises walked very slowly indeed. Not one of them ran!

Mrs. Crawl came slowly to meet Dinah and Mr. Crawl. She did not look at all astonished to see Dinah.

"This little girl has come to live in Tortoise-town," said Mr. Crawl. "She needs somewhere to live, so I have brought her home."

"Welcome!" said Mrs. Crawl, and patted Dinah on the back with a clawed foot. "I expect you are hungry, aren't you? We will soon have dinner! Can you smell it cooking?"

Dinah could and it smelt delicious. "Sit down and I will get dinner," said Mrs. Crawl. Dinah sat down and watched Mrs. Crawl get out a tablecloth.

It took her a long time to open the drawer. It took her even longer to shake out the cloth. It took her simply ages to lay it on the table!

Then she began to lay the table with knives and forks and spoons. It took her over half an hour to do this, and poor Dinah began to get more and more hungry.

"Let *me* put out the plates and glasses," she said impatiently, and jumped up. She bustled round the table, putting the things here and there. Mrs. Crawl looked at her crossly.

"Now for goodness' sake don't go rushing about like that! It's bad for tortoises! It's no good getting out of breath and red in the face."

"I'm not a tortoise," said Dinah.

"Well, you soon will be when you have lived here a little while," said Mr. Crawl, who had spent all this time taking off one boot and putting on one slipper. "You'll see – your hair will fall off and you'll be bald like us – and your neck will get wrinkled – and you'll grow a fine hard shell."

Dinah stared at him in dismay. "I don't want to grow into a tortoise!" she said. "I think you look awful."

Mr. and Mrs. Crawl gazed at Dinah in great annoyance. "Rude little girl," said Mrs. Crawl. "Go and wash your hands – Mr. Crawl will go and wash his first and show you where to run the water."

It took five minutes for Mr. Crawl to walk to the washplace. It took him ten minutes to wash and dry himself, and by that time Mrs. Crawl had actually got the dinner on the table. Dinah was so hungry that she washed her hands more quickly than she had ever washed them in her life before!

Oh dear – *what* a long time Mr. and Mrs. Crawl took over their soup. Dinah finished hers long before they were halfway through, and then had to sit and wait, feeling dreadfully hungry, whilst they finished. She fidgeted, and the two tortoises were cross.

"What an impatient child! Don't fidget so! Learn to be slower, for goodness' sake! You wanted to come and live with us, didn't you? Well, be patient and slow and careful."

Dinner wasn't finished till four o'clock. "Almost tea-time!" thought Dinah. "This is simply dreadful. I know now how horrid it must be for everyone when I am slow at home or at school. They must feel as annoyed and impatient as I do now."

"I'll take you out for a walk when I'm ready," said Mrs. Crawl. "There's a circus on in the market-place, which perhaps you would like to see."

"Oh yes, I would!" cried Dinah. "Oh, do hurry up, Mrs. Crawl. I'm sure that by the time you've got your bonnet on, and your shawl, the circus will have gone!"

"Nobody ever says 'Do hurry up!' in Tortoise-town," said Mrs. Crawl, shocked. "We all take our own time over everything. It's good to be slow. We never run, we never do anything quickly at all. You must learn to be much, much slower, dear child."

It was six o'clock by the time that Mrs. Crawl had got on her bonnet, changed her shoes and put on a nice shawl. Dinah thought that she had never in her life seen anyone so slow. Sometimes Mrs. Crawl would stop what she was doing, and

sit and stare into the air for quite a long time.

"Don't dream!" cried Dinah. "Do hurry up!" And then she remembered how very, very often people had cried out the same thing to her, crossly and impatiently. "What a tiresome nuisance I must have been!" she thought. "I didn't like hurrying up, but I hate even more this having to be *so* slow!"

The circus was just closing down when they reached it. The roundabout was starting for the very last time. Dinah could have cried with disappointment. She got on to a horse, and the roundabout began to play. It turned round very slowly indeed.

Dinah looked at all the creepy-crawly tortoises standing about, looking so solemn and slow, and she couldn't bear them.

"Oh, I wish I was back home!" she cried. "I wish I was! I'd never be slow again, never!"

The roundabout horse that she was riding suddenly neighed loudly. Dinah almost fell off in surprise. It turned its head and looked at her. "I'm a wishing-horse!" it said. "Didn't you know? Be careful what you wish!"

The roundabout went faster. It went very fast. Then it slowed down and stopped – and hey presto, what a surprise! Dinah was no longer in Tortoise-town, but in a field at the bottom of her own garden! She knew it at once. She jumped off the horse and ran to the gate in her own garden wall. She looked back at the roundabout – and it slowly faded like smoke, and then it wasn't there any more.

Dinah tore up the garden path. She rushed up the stairs to the nursery. Her mother was there, and stared in amazement. She had never seen Dinah hurry herself before!

"What's happened to you?" she asked. "You're really being quick for once."

"I've been to Tortoise-town!" said Dinah. "And now I'm back again, hurrah! I'll never be a slow-coach or a tortoise again, never, never, never!"

She probably won't. Is there anyone you know that ought to go to Tortoise-town? Not you, I hope!

Brer Rabbit is So Cunning

ONCE, when Brer Rabbit was trotting along over a field, the wind blew some dead leaves out of the ditch into his face. Brer Rabbit got a real fright, and he tore off as if a hundred dogs were after him!

Well, it happened that Brer Fox and Brer Bear saw him running away, and they laughed to think that a few leaves had frightened Brer Rabbit. They went about among all the animals, telling them what a coward Brer Rabbit was, and how he had run away because of a few leaves.

When people met Brer Rabbit after that, they grinned slyly, and asked him whether he had had any more frights, and Brer Rabbit got very tired of it.

"I'm as brave as any of you!" he said. "And braver too!"

"Well, show us what a brave man you are, then!" cried every one, and they giggled at Brer Rabbit's angry face.

Brer Rabbit went off in a temper, and he thought and thought how he might show every one that he was a brave fellow. Then he grinned and slapped his knee.

"I'll soon show them!" he chuckled. "My, they'll get a fright, but it will serve them right!"

Then Brer Rabbit went to work out his idea. He took seven of his tin plates, made a hole in the middle of each, and threaded them together on a thick string. My, what a noise they made when he shook the string!

Then he took a big piece of glass from his greenhouse and ran his wet paw up and down it to see if it would make a good noise. It did! Oh, what a squeaking, squealing noise it made! Brer Rabbit grinned to himself.

Well, that night Brer Rabbit took the string of tin plates and the piece of glass with him, and climbed up a tree not far from Brer Fox's house. When he was comfortably settled, he began to enjoy himself.

He moaned and howled like twenty cats. He yelped like a dozen dogs. He screeched like a hundred parrots. "Oh-ee-oo-ee, ie-oh-ee-oh, YOW, YOW, YOW!"

Then he shook the string hard that joined the tin plates together, and they all jangled through the quiet night as if a thousand dustbins had gone mad and were dancing in a ring. "Clang, jang, clang, jang, clinky, clanky, clang, JANG!"

Brer Rabbit nearly fell out of the tree with laughing at the awful noise he made. Next, he took the big piece of glass, wetted his paw, and began to run it up and down the glass.

"EEEEEEEE-OOOO, EEEEEEEE-OOOO!" it went, and all the wakened animals round about shivered and shook to hear such a dreadful squealing noise.

Then Brer Rabbit jangled his plates again. "Clang, jang, clang, jang, clinky, clanky, clang, jang!"

Brer Fox was sitting up in bed, as scared as could be. He couldn't for the life of him imagine what the noise was.

Brer Wolf was hiding under his bed. Brer Bear and Mrs. Bear were clinging together, crying on each other's shoulders, there were so frightened.

All the other animals were trembling, too, wondering what was going to happen next.

"Yow, yow, yow!" yelled Brer Rabbit. "Clinkity, clang, jang!" went his tin plates. "EeeeeeEEeeeeEEE-ooooo!" went his paw, squeaking up the glass.

At last Brer Rabbit hopped down his tree, ran to a tumble-down shed nearby, put all his things there, and then made his way to Brer Fox's house. He knocked loudly on the door, "BLIM, BLAM!"

Brer Fox got such a shock that he fell out of bed. "Who's there?" he said in a trembling voice.

"Me, Brer Rabbit," said Brer Rabbit. "I've come to see what all the noise is about."

"Oh, Brer Rabbit, dear Brer Rabbit, I'm so glad to see you," said Brer Fox, almost falling over himself to open the door. "Do come in. I've been scared out of my life. Whatever is that noise, do you think?"

"I don't know," said Brer Rabbit untruthfully. "Unless it is old Brer Elephant rampaging round, making a frightful noise. I just came along to see if you were all right, Brer Fox."

"Well, that's mighty kind of you, Brer Rabbit," said Brer Fox. "I wonder you're not afraid to be out, with all that noise around. What are you going to do now? Don't leave me!"

"I'm just off to see if Brer Wolf and Brer Bear are all right," said Brer Rabbit. "Maybe they are scared and will be glad to see me."

Off he went, and found Brer Wolf and Brer Bear just as scared as Brer Fox. My, they thought he was a very brave fellow to be out that night!

"We'll look in the morning and see if we can see any signs of old Brer Elephant," said Brer Rabbit. "It's a wet, muddy night and maybe we'll find his footprints. Then we can follow them and see where he is!"

After Brer Rabbit had left his friends, he skipped and danced with glee, and then he went to where he had hidden a big round log of wood, just the shape of an elephant's great foot. Brer Rabbit went all round about Brer Fox's house and Brer Bear's and Brer Wolf's, stamping the end of the big log into the mud, so that it looked for all the world as if a mighty big lot of feet had been going around there in the night.

Brer Rabbit giggled to himself when he had finished. He went back home to bed and slept well till the morning.

The next day he and all the other animals went to look for footprints. When the others saw the enormous marks in the mud they were as scared as could be.

"Those are elephant's footprints all right!" said Brer Fox. "I know elephant's marks when I see them. My, he was around here last night all right. I wonder he didn't knock my house down!"

"Let's follow the footprints," said Brer Rabbit.

"I don't think I want to do that," said Brer Bear, who didn't like the look of things at all.

"What! Are you afraid?" cried Brer Rabbit. "Well, *I'm* not! I'm going to see where these footmarks lead to, even if I have to go alone!"

Well, he followed the footprints in the mud, and they led him to the old tumbledown shed, as he knew they would, for he had put them there himself! Brer Fox and the others followed him at a good distance. Brer Rabbit tiptoed to the shed and looked inside.

He tiptoed back to the others at once. "Yes," said the cunning fellow, "he's in there all right! Fast asleep! I think I'll go and attack him whilst he's asleep!"

"What! Attack an elephant!" said Brer Wolf in the greatest astonishment. "Don't be silly."

"*I'm* not afraid of elephants!" said Brer Rabbit. "I'll just go in and bang him on the head! I guess he'll rush out in a mighty hurry, so be careful he doesn't knock you all over!"

"Come back, Brer Rabbit!" called Brer Fox, as Brer Rabbit tiptoed to the shed again. "You'll only make him angry, and he'll rush out and knock down all our houses!"

Brer Rabbit disappeared into the shed. He had a good laugh and then he began. He took up his string of tin plates and made them dance with a clanky-lanky clang-jang! He made his paw squeal up and down the glass. He yowled and howled. He took a tin trumpet from his pocket and blew hard, for he had once heard that elephants made a trumpeting sound.

Then he began to shout and yell in his own voice, "Take *that*, you great noisy creature! Take *that*, you stupid elephant! And that, and that, and that!"

Every time he said, "And *that!*" Brer Rabbit hit the side of the shed with a piece of wood and it made a terrible noise. Crash! Crash! Crash!

The animals waiting not far off shivered and shook. Brer Rabbit put his eye to a crack in the wall of the shed and grinned to see them.

Then he took a heap of paper bags out of his pocket, and blew them up one by one. He banged them with his hand and they went, POP!

POP! POP! POP! POP! They sounded like guns shooting. Brer Rabbit jangled his plates again, and banged the shed with the piece of wood. You might have thought that at least twenty animals were fighting inside that shed!

And then Brer Rabbit took up the log that he had made the footprints with and sent it crashing through the other side of the shed, as if some big animal had fallen through it and was scrambling away. He began to shout.

"Run, Brer Elephant, run!" he yelled. "Run, or I'll get you! Run, run!"

Brer Fox, Brer Wolf, and all the others thought that the elephant had crashed its way out of the shed and was loose. At once they fled to Brer Fox's house and bolted themselves in, trembling. Brer Rabbit saw them from the crack in the shed and laughed fit to kill himself.

When at last he stopped laughing he made his way to Brer Fox's house, panting as if he had been having a great fight. He knocked at the door, "blam, blam!"

"Who's there?" called Brer Fox, afraid.

"Brer Rabbit," said Brer Rabbit in a big voice. The door opened and all the animals came out. They crowded round Brer Rabbit, patted him on the back, hugged him and fussed him! My, it was grand for Brer Rabbit!

"You're a hero!" cried Brer Fox.

"The bravest creature in the world!" said Brer Bear.

"The strongest of us all!" said Brer Wolf.

"I'm glad you think so, friends," said Brer Rabbit. "There was a time when you called me a coward, and maybe if I remember which of you laughed at me then, I might treat them as I treated old Brer Elephant!"

"*We* wouldn't laugh at a brave man like Brer Rabbit!" shouted every one at once.

"Well, just see you don't!" said Brer Rabbit, and he put his nose in the air, threw out his chest, and walked off, looking mighty biggitty! And after that the animals were very careful to be polite to Brer Rabbit for a long, long time!

The Little Singing Kettle

Mr. Curly was a small pixie who lived all by himself in Twisty Cottage. His cottage stood at the end of the Village of Ho, and was always very neatly kept. It had blue and yellow curtains at the windows and blue and yellow flowers in the garden, so you can guess how pretty and trim it was.

Mr. Curly was mean. He was the meanest pixie that ever lived, but he always pretended to be very generous indeed. If he had a bag of peppermints he never let anyone see it, but put it straight into his pocket till he got home. And if he met any of the other pixies he would pull a long face and say:

"If only I had a bag of sweets I would offer you one."

"Never mind," the others said. "It's nice of you to think of it!"

And they went off, saying what a nice, generous creature Mr. Curly was!

Now one day, as Mr. Curly was walking home along Dimity Lane, where the trees met overhead, so that it was just like walking in a green tunnel, he saw a strange person in front of him. This was a Humpy Goblin, and he carried a great many saucepans, kettles and pans all slung down his back, round his shoulders and over his chest.

They made a great noise as he walked, but louder than the noise was the Humpy Goblin's voice. He sang all the time in a voice like a cracked bell.

"Do you want a saucepan, kettle or pan?
If you do, here's the Goblin Man!
The Humpy Goblin with his load
Of pots and pans is down the road,
Hie, hie, hie, here's the Goblin Man,
Do you want a saucepan, kettle or pan?"

Now Mr. Curly badly wanted a new kettle, because his own had a hole in it and the water leaked over his stove each day, making a funny hissing noise. So he ran after the Goblin Man and called him. The Humpy Goblin turned round and grinned. He was a cheerful fellow, always pleased to see anybody.

"I want a good little kettle, nice and cheap," said Curly.

"I've just the one for you," said Humpy, and he pointed to a bright little kettle on his back. Curly looked at it.

"How much is it?" he asked.

"Sixpence," said the Goblin. This was quite cheap, but mean old Curly wasn't going to give sixpence for the kettle. He pretended to be shocked at the price, and then he gave a huge sigh.

"Oh, I'm not rich enough to pay all that," he said sadly. "I can only pay threepence."

"Oh, no," said Humpy firmly. "Threepence isn't enough. You must pay sixpence."

Well, they stood and talked to one another for a long time, one saying sixpence and the other saying threepence, until at last the Humpy Goblin laughed in Curly's face and walked off jingling all his kettles and pans.

"You're a mean old stick!" he called after Curly. "I'm not going to sell you anything! Good-bye, Mr. Mean!"

Off he went and soon began to sing his song again. Curly heard him.

"Do you want a saucepan, kettle or pan?
If you do, here's the Goblin Man!"

Curly stood and watched him angrily. Then he started walking, too. He had to follow the Goblin Man because that was the way home to Twisty Cottage. But he took care not to follow too close, for he was afraid that Humpy might call something rude after him.

It was a hot day and the Goblin was tired. After a while he thought he would sit down in the hedge and rest. So down he sat – and it wasn't more than a minute before he was sound asleep and snoring! Curly heard him and knew he must be asleep. A naughty thought slipped into his head.

"I wonder if I could take that kettle from him whilst he's asleep! I could leave threepence beside him to pay for it. How cross he would be when he woke up to find that I had got the kettle for threepence after all!"

He crept up to the Humpy Goblin. He certainly was sound asleep, with his mouth so wide open that it was a good thing there wasn't anything above his head that could drop into it. Curly carefully undid the little shining kettle without making even a clink of noise. Then he put three bright pennies on the grass beside the Goblin, and ran off, chuckling to himself for being so smart.

He soon reached home. He filled the little kettle with water and put it on the fire. It really was a dear little thing, and it boiled very quickly indeed, sending a spurt of steam out of the spout almost before Curly had got out the teapot to make the tea.

Just as he was sitting down to enjoy a cup of tea and a piece of cake, someone walked up his garden path and looked in at the door. It was the Humpy Goblin. When he saw that Curly had the kettle on the fire, he grinned all over his face.

"So you've got it!" he said. "Well, much good may it do you! Kettle, listen to me! Teach Mr. Curly the lesson he needs! Ho, ho, Curly, keep the kettle! I don't want it!

Laughing and skipping, the Goblin went down the path again. Curly felt a bit uncomfortable. What was he laughing like that for?

"Oh, he just tried to frighten me and make me think something nasty would happen," said Curly to himself. "Silly old Goblin!"

He cleared away his cup and saucer, and filled up the kettle again. He was washing up the dirty dishes when a knock came at his door, and Dame Pitapat looked in.

"I say, Curly, could you let me have a little tea? I've emptied my tin and it's such a long way to the shops."

Now Curly had a whole tin full, but he wasn't going to let Dame Pitapat have any. He ran to the dresser and took down a tin he knew was empty.

"Yes, certainly, Dame Pitapat," he said, "you shall have some of my tea. Oh, dear! The tin's empty! What a pity! You could have had half of it if only I'd had any, but I must have used it all up!"

Dame Pitapat looked at the empty tin. Then she turned to go.

"I'm sorry I bothered you, Curly," she said. "It was kind of you to say I could have had half, if only you'd had any tea."

Then a funny thing happened. The little kettle on the stove sent out a big spurt of steam and began to sing a shrill song.

"Mr. Curly has plenty of tea!
He's just as mean as a pixie can be!
Look in the tin on the left of the shelf
And see what a lot he has for himself!"

Then the kettle took another breath and shouted, "Mean old thing! Stingy old thing! Oooooh, look at him!"

Dame Pitapat was so astonished that she stood gaping for quite a minute. She couldn't think where the song came from. She had no idea it was the kettle on the stove. But Curly knew it was, and he was so angry and ashamed that he could have cried.

Dame Pitapat went to the shelf and took down the tin that stood on the left. She opened it, and sure enough, it was full to the brim of tea.

"Oh, look at this!" she said. "Well, Curly, you said I could have half of any tea you had, so I shall take you at your word. Thanks very much." She emptied half the tea out into the tin she had brought and went out of the cottage, looking round curiously to see if she could spy who had sung that song about Curly. But she didn't think of looking at the kettle, of course.

Curly was so angry with the kettle that he decided to beat it with a stick. But before he could do that someone poked his head in at the window and called him.

"Mr. Curly! Will you lend me your umbrella, please? I've lost mine and it's raining."

It was little Capers, the pixie who lived next door. He was always lending Curly things, and now he had come to borrow something himself. But Curly was in a very bad temper.

"My umbrella's lost too," he said. "I'm so sorry, Capers. You could have it if only I had it myself, but it's gone."

"Oh, well, never mind," said Capers. "It's nice of you to say you would have lent it to me."

Before he could go the shining kettle gave a tiny hop on the stove and began to sing again.

"Mr. Curly has got an umbrella,
He's such a mean and stingy fella,
He says he hasn't got one at all
But just you go and look in the hall!"

Then it took another breath and began to shout again at the top of its steamy voice, "Mean old thing! Stingy old thing! Oooooh, look at him!"

Capers was so surprised to hear this song that he nearly fell in at the window. He stared at Curly, who was looking as black as thunder and as red as a beetroot. Then Capers looked through the kitchen door into the tiny hall – and sure enough Curly's green umbrella stood there.

Capers jumped in at the window and fetched the umbrella. He waved it at Curly.

"You said I could have it if only you had got it!" he cried. "Here it is, so I'll borrow it! Many thanks!"

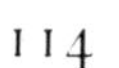

He ran off and left Curly nearly crying with rage. The pixie caught up a stick and ran to beat the kettle – but that small kettle was far too quick for him! It rose up in the air and put itself high up on a shelf for safety. Then it poured just a drop of boiling water on to Curly's hand, which made the pixie dance and shout with pain.

"You wait till I get you!" cried Curly, shaking his stick.

Someone knocked at his front door. Curly opened it. Rag and Tag, the two gnomes, stood there smiling.

"Mr. Curly, we are collecting pennies for poor Mr. Tumble whose house was burnt down yesterday," they said. "You are so generous that we thought you would be sure to give us one."

Curly knew that there was no money in his pockets, so he pulled them inside out quickly, saying, "Oh yes, you shall have whatever money I have, Rag and Tag. Goodness, there's none in this pocket – and none in that! How unfortunate! I haven't any pennies to give you, and I should have been *so* pleased to let you have all I had."

"Well, that's very nice of you to say so," said Rag and Tag. "Never mind. Thank you very much for *trying* to be generous!" But before they could go, the little kettle was singing again, spurting out great clouds of steam as it did so!

"Although he says he hasn't any,
Curly's got a silver penny!
Look in his purse on the table there
And take the money he well can spare!"

Then, taking another breath, the kettle shouted with all its might, "Mean old thing! Stingy old thing! Oooooh, look at him!"

Rag and Tag stared all round the kitchen to see where the voice came from, but they couldn't see anyone but Curly. It couldn't be the pixie singing, surely! No, he looked too angry to sing anything!

The gnomes saw the purse lying on the table and they ran for it. Inside was a silver sixpence. They took it and put it into their box.

"Well, Curly," they said, "you said we might have any pennies you had, if you'd had any – and you have, so we'll take this silver one. Good-bye!"

Out they went, giggling together, wondering who it was in the cottage that had given Curly away.

As for Curly, he was so angry that he took a jug of milk and flung it straight at the kettle, which was still high up on the shelf. Crash! The kettle hopped aside and the jug broke in to a dozen pieces against the wall behind. The milk spilt and dripped on to Curly's head. Then the kettle began to laugh. How it laughed! It was a funny, wheezy laugh, but you can't think how angry it made Curly!

He took up a hammer and flung that at the kettle too – but once more it slipped to one side, and oh, dear me, smash went a lovely big jar of plum jam up on the shelf. It all splashed down on to Curly, so what with milk and jam he was a fine sight. The kettle nearly killed itself with laughing. It almost fell off the shelf.

Curly went and washed himself under the tap. He felt frightened. What was he going to do with that awful singing kettle? He must get rid of it somehow or it would tell everyone the most dreadful tales about him.

"I'll wait till to-night," thought Curly. "Then, when it's asleep, I'll take it and throw it away."

So he took no more notice of the kettle, and as no more visitors came that day the kettle was fairly quiet – except that sometimes it would suddenly shout, "Mean old thing! Stingy old thing! Oooooooh, look at him!" The Curly would almost jump out of his skin with fright, and glare at the kettle angrily.

At nine o'clock Curly went to bed. The kettle hopped down to the stove and went to sleep. Curly waited for a little while and then he crept out of bed. He went to the stove and took hold of the kettle. Ah, he had it now! The kettle woke up and shouted, but Curly had it by the handle. The water in it was no longer hot, so that it could not hurt Curly.

The pixie hurried outside with the kettle and went to the bottom of his garden. There was a rubbish-heap there and the pixie stuffed the struggling kettle right into the middle. He left it there and went back delighted. He climbed into bed and fell asleep.

But at midnight something woke him by tapping at the window.

"Let me in!" cried a voice. "Let me in! I'm dirty and I want washing!"

"That's that horrid kettle!" thought Curly, in a fright. "Well, it can go on tapping! I won't let it in!"

But the kettle tapped and tapped and at last it flung itself hard against the glass, broke it and came in through the hole! It went over to Curly's bed and stood itself there.

"Wash me!" it said. "I'm dirty and smelly. You shouldn't have put me on that nasty rubbish-heap!"

"Get out of my nice clean bed!" cried Curly angrily. "Looking what a mess you are making!"

But the kettle wouldn't get off, and in the end the angry pixie had to get up and wash the kettle till it was clean again. Then he banged it down on the stove and left it.

Next day the kettle sang songs about him again, and Curly kept hearing it shout, "Mean old fellow! Stingy old fellow! Ooooooh, look at him!" till he was tired of it. So many people had heard about the strange things happening in the pixie's cottage that all day long visitors came to ask for different things, and poor Curly was nearly worried out of his life.

"I'll drown that kettle in my well to-night!" he thought. So once more he took the kettle when it was asleep and threw it down the well. Splash! Ha, it wouldn't get out of there in a hurry!

But about three o'clock in the morning there came a tap-tap-tap at the window, which had now been mended. It was the kettle back again!

"Curly! Let me in! I'm c-c-c-c-cold and w-wet! Let me in!"

Curley was afraid his window would be broken again, so he jumped out of bed and let in the shivering kettle. To his horror it crept into bed with him and wouldn't go away!

"It was cold and wet in the well!" said the kettle. "Warm me, Curly!"

So Curly had to warm the kettle, and how angry he was! It was so uncomfortable to sleep with a kettle, especially one that kept sticking its sharp spout into him. But he had to put up with it. In the morning he put the kettle back on the stove and started to think hard whilst he had his breakfast.

"I can't get rid of that kettle," he said to himself. "And while it's here it's sure to sing horrid things about me every time anyone comes to borrow something. I wonder what it would do if I let people have what they ask for? I'll try and see."

So when Mother Homey came and begged for a bit of soap because she had run out of it and the shops were closed that afternoon Curly gave her a whole new piece without making any excuse at all. Mother Homey was surprised and delighted.

"Thank you so much," she said. "You're a kind soul, Curly."

The kettle said nothing at all. Not a single word. As for Curly, he suddenly felt very nice inside. It was lovely to give somebody something. It made him feel warm and kind. He made up his mind to do it again if he felt nice the next time – and to see if the wretched kettle said anything.

He soon found that the kettle said never a word unless he was mean or untruthful – and he found, too, that it was lovely to be kind and to give things away; it was nice even to lend them.

"I've been horrid and nasty," thought Curly to himself. "I'll turn over a new leaf and try to be different. And that old kettle can say what it likes! Anyway, it boils very quickly and makes a lovely pot of tea."

Very soon the kettle found little to say, for Curly became kind and generous. Once or twice he forgot, but as soon as he heard the kettle beginning to speak he quickly remembered, and the kettle stopped its song.

And one day who should peep in at the door but the Humpy Goblin, grinning all over his face as usual.

"Hallo, Curly!" he said. "How did you like the kettle? Was it cheap for threepence? I've come to take it back, if you want to get rid of it. It was a mean trick to play on you, really, but I think you deserved it!"

Curly looked at the smiling Goblin. Then he took his purse from his pocket and found three pennies. He held them out to the Humpy Goblin.

"Here you are," he said. "You wanted sixpence for the kettle and I was mean enough to leave you only threepence. Here's the other threepence."

"But – but – don't you want to give me back the kettle?" asked Humpy in surprise. "I left a horrid singing spell in it."

"Yes, I know," said Curly. "But I deserved it. I'm different now. I like the kettle too – we're great friends. I try to be kind now, so the kettle doesn't sing nasty things about me. It just hums nice, friendly little songs."

"Well, well, well, wonders will never end!" said the Goblin Man, astonished. "Don't bother about the other threepence, Curly. I don't want it."

"Well, if you won't take it, let me offer you a cup of tea made from water boiled in the singing kettle," said Curly. Humpy was even more astonished to hear the pixie being so kind, but he sat down at the table in delight.

Then he and Curly had a cup of tea each and a large slice of ginger cake – and the talked together and found that they liked one another very much indeed.

So now Mr. Curly and the Humpy Goblin are the very greatest friends, and the little singing kettle hums its loudest when it boils water for their tea. You should just hear it!

Dame Roundy's Stockings

DAME ROUNDY was a clever old woman. She made Lucky Stockings of red, green, yellow, purple, orange and brown. Whoever wore her Lucky Stockings would be sure to have good luck for a whole day. So you can guess that Dame Roundy sold plenty, and there were always elves, pixies, gnomes and goblins in and out of her front door, coming to buy her Lucky Stockings.

But she would never sell her Lucky Stockings to witches or wizards. "No," she would say, "I don't trust witches or wizards. They sometimes use bad magic instead of good. I don't want them to have my Lucky Stockings."

So the wizard who lived in Windy Wood nearby had to go without a pair of Lucky Stockings, although nearly everyone else had them. He was called Wizard Shaggy because he had such big black eyebrows. He was not really a bad wizard, but he wasn't kind or generous as most of the people around were.

One day he badly wanted some Lucky Stockings. He had had weeks of bad luck, when everything had gone wrong that could go wrong. His chimney had smoked, and the sweep wouldn't come. He had fallen down and hurt both his knees badly. He had had a bad cold, and somehow or other he had made himself the wrong Sneezing-Spell, and instead of stopping his sneezing the spell had made him sneeze two hundred times without stopping, which was very tiring.

"I simply *must* have some good luck!" said the Shaggy Wizard to himself. "I shall go and ask Dame Roundy to sell me some Lucky Stockings – and, if she won't, I shall get them *somehow*!"

So he went to ask her. But she shook her head. "You know my rule, Shaggy," She said. "No Lucky Stockings for witches or wizards! So go away."

Now, that night Shaggy went quietly to Dame Roundy's and listened to see if she was asleep. She was. He could hear her snoring very gently, and he grinned to himself.

He knew where she kept her Lucky Stockings. She had a big red box, and into this she popped each Lucky Stocking as soon as she had finished knitting it.

Shaggy tried the kitchen window. It wasn't locked. He opened it very, very quietly. He climbed over the sill into the kitchen. He felt his way to the red box. He opened it and took out as many stockings as he could hold. He only wanted one pair – but he thought he could easily sell the others to wizards and witches, who were always longing for them and could never get them.

He shut the box. He climbed back into the garden. He shut the window. Then he rushed off to Windy Wood as fast as he could go. Hurray! He had plenty of Lucky Stockings now, and he would soon get some good luck.

But when he got back to his cottage he began to feel rather uncomfortable. Suppose Dame Roundy guessed he had stolen them? She might send Burly, the village policeman, to search his house. Certainly he wouldn't dare to wear any of the stockings for some time in case people noticed that he had a new pair, and told Dame Roundy.

"I haven't been so clever as I thought," said Shaggy to himself. "I'll have to hide the stockings somewhere so that no one will know where they are!"

He looked at the pile of brightly-coloured stockings, and scratched his head. Where should he hide them?

"I know!" he said suddenly. "I'll go and hang them up in the trees! Their leaves are all colours now – red, and brown, and yellow and orange – and the bright stockings will match them beautifully. No one will guess they are hanging up in the trees among the bright autumn leaves!"

So out went Shaggy to do what he had planned. Soon all the coloured stockings were carefully hidden among the leafy branches of the nearby trees. Then Shaggy went to bed, feeling quite certain that nobody would guess his secret.

In the morning Dame Roundy was amazed and angry to find her stockings stolen. She at once sent for Burly, the policeman.

"Shaggy the Wizard came to ask for some of my Lucky Stockings yesterday," said Dame Roundy. "I think you should ask him a few questions, Burly."

So off went Burly to see Wizard Shaggy – and on the way what did he find but a yellow Lucky Stocking, dropped on the path that led to Shaggy's cottage! Then Burly felt quite certain that Shaggy had taken those stockings and had hidden them away.

Shaggy pretended to be very surprised to see Burly, and he told him a lot of naughty stories.

"No, I didn't take the stockings. No, I shouldn't dream of doing such a thing! No, I wasn't out last night, I was fast asleep all night through. I certainly haven't hidden the stockings. You just hunt around my cottage and see if you can find a single one!"

Burly did hunt, but of course he couldn't find any of the stockings. He looked in the shed outside. He looked down the well. In fact, he looked everywhere, even up the chimney, but he couldn't see a sign of those Lucky Stockings.

And yet he felt quite certain that Shaggy had them. Still, he had to go home at last, and Shaggy grinned like anything to see the back of him!

"Nobody will ever find my clever hiding-place!" he said.

But that night a frost came. It was a very hard frost, and it loosened all the autumn leaves on the trees. In the morning the wind got up and blew hard. The leaves, which had been made very loose by the frost, began to flutter down in the wind.

Down came the leaves and down and down. Soon they were ankle-deep in the wood. A crowd of pixies, coming home from school, shuffled through the leaves happily.

"The trees are almost bare," said one, looking up. Then he stared hard. "I say – what are those things in that tree up there! And look, there are some more over there – in that bare chestnut tree! And some more in that hazel tree! Are they funny long leaves?"

Everyone stared. "They look like stockings!" said another pixie.

"They *are* stockings!" said a third. "Dame Roundy's stockings – the ones that were stolen. They've been hidden in the trees. Quick, quick, come and tell Burly and Dame Roundy."

The pixies rushed off, and soon came back with Burly and Dame Roundy. While the pixies had been gone, Shaggy had suddenly noticed that all the leaves had fallen off the trees, and that the hidden stockings were now flapping and waving wildly in the strong wind. Anyone could see them!

In a great fright he rushed out and began to get the stockings down – and, just as he was doing that, up came Dame Roundy, and Burly the policeman!

"So you *were* the thief, and you *did* hide the stockings!" cried Burly, getting hold of Shaggy and shaking him till his hat flew off. "Well, you can just come along with me now. I've got a few things to say to you!"

"Oh, I thought I was so clever, hiding the stockings among the bright leaves!" wailed Shaggy.

"I suppose you forgot that leaves fall off in the autumn!" said Dame Roundy, collecting all her stockings. "Well, for a wizard, I must say you are really very stupid. Even a five-year-old child could have told you that!"

"What punishment shall we give him?" cried Burly.

"Let him come to me and learn to knit Lucky Stockings!" said Dame Roundy, with a smile. "It will be a good lesson for him to knit Lucky Stockings for other people and never be allowed to wear any himself!"

So that is what Shaggy *is* doing now – and he *does* have to work hard. Dame Roundy sees to that. If *you* want a pair of Lucky Stockings, you'll know where to go, but you have to be a good, kind person or Dame Roundy won't sell you any.

The Nice Juicy Carrot

In the field at the back of the farm lived three grey donkeys. They were called Neddy, Biddy and Hee-Haw. Sometimes the farmer put one into the harness belonging to a small carriage, and his little daughter drove out for a ride. But usually the donkeys didn't have much to do, and they very often quarrelled.

One day Neddy found a large juicy carrot in the ditch, and he was most excited about it. In fact, he was so excited that instead of keeping quiet about it and nibbling it till it was gone, he raised his head and cried: "Eeyore! Eeyore! Eeyore!"

Just like that.

Well, of course, the other two donkeys came running up to see what was the matter, and they saw the nice juicy carrot too. And they wanted to eat it.

But Neddy put his thick little body in the way and said: "No, that's my carrot."

Biddy tried to scrape the carrot near her with her foot.

"It's *my* carrot!" she said.

"I'm the hungriest, so it's *my* carrot!" said Hee-Haw, and he tried to push the others away.

Then Neddy saw that he would not be allowed to eat it in peace, and he thought of a plan to decide which donkey should have the carrot. "Let us see who can bray the loudest," he said.

So they began. First Neddy brayed.

"Eeyore, eeyore, eeyore!" he cried, and a little sandy rabbit running not far off was so astonished at the loud noise that he came near to see what it was all about.

Then Biddy brayed. "EEYORE, EEYORE, EEYORE!" she cried, and the watching rabbit thought it a very ugly noise.

Then Hee-Haw brayed, and his voice was so loud that a hedgehog not far off was frightened almost out of his life, and curled himself up into a tight ball.

"EEYORE, EEYORE, EEYORE!" roared Hee-Haw. The listening rabbit thought that donkeys had terrible voices. Then, dear me, the rabbit caught sight of that nice juicy carrot lying just nearby in the ditch. How his nose twitched when he saw it!

He crept out from his hiding-place and the three donkeys saw him. "Look! There is a rabbit!" cried Hee-Haw. "He shall tell us which brayed the loudest just now. Then we shall know who wins the carrot!"

So they called to the rabbit to judge between them. But the bunny was very artful. He didn't want to see the carrot eaten by a donkey. So he looked wisely at the three grey animals and shook his head.

"There wasn't much to choose between your braying," he said. "Why don't you have a race? Then you could easily tell who should have the carrot."

"That's a good idea," said the donkeys. "Where shall we race to, rabbit?"

"Oh, all round the field and back again to where I sit," answered the wily rabbit. "Now, are you ready? One, two, three, off!"

Away went the three donkeys at top speed. Round the field they went at a gallop, much to the astonishment of the farmer's wife. They panted and puffed, kicking up their heels in fine style, each trying to get ahead of the other.

They all arrived back at the starting-place at the same moment. But each donkey thought it had won.

"I've won!" said Neddy.

"No, I'm first!" brayed Biddy.

"The carrot's mine!" roared Hee-Haw.

"Let's ask the rabbit who's won," said Neddy. "He'll know."

So they called to the rabbit – but there was no answer. They called again, and still they had no reply. Then they looked for the carrot.

It was gone!

Pipkin Plays a Trick

Pipkin and Penny were very pleased with themselves. They were two pixies who lived in a neat house in the middle of Chuckle Village. They had just finished making a beautiful gravel path that stretched right from their front door to their gate, quite a long way. It was a nice wide path, made of fine yellow gravel.

"It ought to be watered and rolled now," said Pipkin. "We've shovelled down the gravel, but it's very rough to the feet. If we water it and roll it well, it will be lovely."

So they went to get their watering-can and their roller. The watering-can was all right, but alas, their roller was broken! It was no use at all.

"We must borrow one," said Penny. "Mr. Grip has a nice one. Let's go and ask him to lend it to us." So they went to Mr. Grip's house – but he was a surly fellow, and wouldn't lend it.

"No," he said, "I don't lend things to pixies. They are too careless."

"We're *not* careless!" said Pipkin, quite cross. "We always look after things that are lent to us and take them back again."

But Mr. Grip banged his door in their faces and the two pixies had to go.

"We'll ask Dame Roundy if she'll lend us *her* roller," said Penny, hopefully. "Hers is a fine big one."

So off they went to Dame Roundy's. She was making cakes and said she couldn't be bothered to get the key of her garden shed.

"Go and ask someone else," she said, impatiently. "I can't trouble about it now." Pipkin and Penny went away. They thought it was very unkind of Dame Roundy.

"We'll go to the gnome Chiffle-Chuffle," said Pipkin. "His roller is very big indeed."

They knocked at the door of Chiffle-Chuffle's house. There was no answer. But Pipkin suddenly saw the gnome's face peeping through the window at them, and he called him.

"Chiffle-Chuffle, answer the door! We've come to ask you to lend us your big roller." The gnome slipped his head inside and made no answer. He was pretending not to be in. He didn't want to lend his roller to the pixies.

Pipkin and Penny knocked as loudly as they could once more, for they knew quite well that Chiffle-Chuffle was at home – but it was no good, he wouldn't open the door. So off they went down the garden-path, very angry with Chiffle-Chuffle for being so mean.

"There's only Mrs. Tippitty left who's got a roller," said Penny. "Oh, I do hope she will lend it to us. She's such a cross old thing that I'm afraid she won't."

He was quite right. Mrs. Tippitty was in a very bad temper that afternoon, and when she heard that the pixies wanted to borrow her roller she went quite purple with rage.

"What, lend my fine roller to two careless pixies like you!" she cried. "Whatever next? No, indeed – and run away quickly before I box your ears!"

You should have seen Pipkin and Penny run! They knew quite well that Mrs. Tippitty meant what she said, for she had often boxed their ears before. They went home and looked sadly at their gravel path. It did so badly want rolling.

And then Pipkin had a great idea. He whispered it to Penny, who was simply delighted.

"When Mr. Grip, Dame Roundy, Chiffle-Chuffle and Mrs. Tippitty come by our cottage to-day on their way back from their shopping we will play your trick on them," said Penny. "It's a clever plan!"

What do you think it was? Ah, you wait and see!

After tea Mr. Grip, Dame Roundy, Chiffle-Chuffle and Mrs. Tippitty all passed by to do their shopping in Chuckle Village. Pipkin and Penny watched them from their window.

"In about half-an-hour they'll be back again," said Pipkin, excited. "Go out and hide that penny of yours down deep in the gravel, Penny."

Penny slipped out and dug a little hole in the new gravel path. He hid a penny there and then carefully covered it up. Then he and Pipkin waited for the shoppers to return. Chiffle-Chuffle came first, carrying a big bag of potatoes.

As soon as the pixies saw him they pretended to be very busy hunting for something in the gravel path. He stopped to ask them if they had lost something.

"There's some money somewhere in the gravel," said Pipkin.

"I'll help you to look for it," said Chiffle-Chuffle, hoping that if he found it the

two pixies would give him some of it for his trouble. So in at the gate he came and began to walk up and down the new gravel path looking for the money. He had enormous feet, and how they crunched the gravel as he walked.

Then Dame Roundy, as plump as her name, and with big galoshes on her feet, peeped over the gate, looking in surprise at the two pixies and the gnome hunting up and down the path.

"What are you looking for?" she asked.

"Money," said Chiffle-Chuffle. "We don't need your help. Go away."

Well, of course, Dame Roundy wasn't going to be ordered away by Chiffle-Chuffle like that! No, she got very red and glared at the gnome in a rage.

"Oh, you want to find the money and keep it for yourself, do you, Chiffle-Chuffle!" she said. "Well, I'll just come in and look too, to see fair play!"

To the pixies' great delight in she came and began to plod up and down the gravel path with her heavy galoshes, looking and looking for the money.

"She's better than a roller!" whispered Pipkin to Penny. "Her galoshes squash the gravel down beautifully!"

Soon along came Mr. Grip and Mrs. Tippitty, walking together. They stopped in surprise when they saw so many people walking up and down the pixies' gravel path.

"Come and help too!" cried Dame Roundy. "We are looking for some money!"

In went Mr. Grip and Mrs. Tippitty, eager to join the fun. Mrs. Tippitty had small feet so she really wasn't much use to press down the gravel, but Mr. Grip had his great wellington boots on, and they were fine for the gravel.

Well, you should have seen them all hunting up and down that gravel path, looking for the money. They didn't know it was only a penny, they just hunted and hunted. And the gravel path got smoother and smoother and smoother, just as if it had been carefully rolled by their rollers! It was fine to see it, and the two pixies couldn't help chuckling.

At last when the path was as smooth as could be, Pipkin and Penny thought it was time for everyone to go.

"Never mind about looking any more," said Penny. "Thank you all very much. You haven't found the money, but you've made our path nice and smooth for us."

Then Mr. Grip, Dame Roundy, Chiffle-Chuffle and Mrs. Tippitty all suddenly remembered that the pixies had asked to borrow their rollers that day – and they looked at the path and saw how their feet had flattened it out nicely, almost as well as a roller would have done. Then they knew that a trick had been played on them and they were angry.

"It's a trick!" cried Mrs. Tippitty.

"There isn't any money in the path!" roared Chiffle-Chuffle.

"It's because we wouldn't lend the pixies our rollers!" shouted Mr. Grip.

"I'll smack them!" said Dame Roundy. But the pixies were too quick for her. They ran into their house and banged the door. Pipkin opened the window and leaned out.

"There *is* some money in the gravel!" he cried. "There really is."

"Tell us where it is, or we'll punish you," said Mr. Grip, shaking his fist.

"Yes, and we'll keep the money too, for our trouble in looking for it!" cried Dame Roundy.

"Well, if we tell you where it is and let you share it between you, will you go away quietly and not worry us any more?" said Penny.

"Yes!" shouted everyone.

"Do you see that red snapdragon leaning over the path just there?" said Penny. "Well, dig up the path a little by it and you'll find the money."

Mr. Grip did as Penny said; and very soon he found the penny. He picked it up and looked at it. When he saw it was only a penny he was so angry that he flung it straight at the two grinning pixies, who had their heads out of the window to see what was happening.

The others, who hadn't seen that it was only a penny, were angry with Mr. Grip for throwing the money to Pipkin and Penny. They ran at him and if he hadn't slipped out of the gate very quickly indeed he would have had his coat pulled right off! He tore down the lane and Dame Roundy, Chiffle-Chuffle and Mrs. Tippitty raced after him.

Pipkin and Penny leaned against one another and laughed till they cried. Then they picked up the penny from the floor and put it into their money-box.

"That will teach Dame Roundy and the others not to be so mean about lending things another time," said Penny, looking out on his nice smooth path.

"Yes, it will," said Pipkin, rubbing his hands together in delight. "They've wasted lots of time in looking for a penny which they didn't get in the end – and they've flattened out our new path for us nicely! Ha ha, ho ho!"

You should see the path. It's the best in Chuckle Village!